I0616459

Copyright

Cover Photo Credit: NASA, James Webb Telescope

Contents

PART ONE

Chapter 1: Group Therapy

POP-P-POP! Before he is even aware, Calvin jumps up to some muffled pops and a tussle outside his door. He stares at the door until it goes silent again, then he starts to breathe heavily and more frequently.

"Shit. I have to calm down— can't over think it, I don't know what that was. I mean, this can't be worse than that heat."

He scrunches his brow and struggles to calm down as he makes white fists. The inhales disrupt the exhales, and several chains of coughs ensues.

Calvin stops and regains his inner functions, then lies back and closes his eyes to engage in a full stretch. He follows that with a tight clinch of his lean frame, and another final stretch. Then, a great exhale. He shuts his mouth and listens to the new silence.

A good-looking biracial man in his mid-30's with a pleasant disposition, Calvin stands at 6'2" and sports a shaved head. He scratches his scruffy stubble while he snatches the light prescription glasses off the end table.

Below the wall-hung television, there's an opened suitcase on the dresser. The closet has a few hangers. His small movements echo as he looks outside at the falling snow on the grass and trees. The light blue light glowing in the window inspires a thought, "Looks so peaceful." He takes his pills from his blue and yellow pill dispenser section marked 'Mo AM' and downs them with a sip of water.

The patient gets up and puts on the white tracksuit and sneakers from the suitcase. There is a knock down the hall as he slips the second shoe on his foot. He looks around his room and goes back to the nightstand to grab his spin-fidgeter.

KNOCK-KNOCK!

He opens the door to two large orderlies. The larger one hands him two earpieces and motions to wear them. Calvin inserts them without an issue, "Yes?"

"Time for therapy," the larger one answers.

"Why am I wearing these earpieces?"

"They'll explain."

The other orderly shuts the door behind Calvin as he gathers himself for a layer of confidence, then they proceed down the hall.

The empty hallway is without flavor or style like plain, old wheat bran. Around a corner, there are two women and a man in line. The orderlies motion for Calvin to get behind them and wait. The others look at Calvin and then at each other in bemusement as a group of orderlies waits nearby.

With the help of a nurse, whose stoic, yet brimming demeanor attracts attention, a silver-haired doctor, with an average build and a calm way, directs the room of people sitting in a circle to get up and move. The circle surrounds an Ottoman sized black box with a small light on top. Patients are more alert than curious as emotional energies seem to run the gamut.

The doctor speaks to Calvin and the three others in the hallway, "Hello, yes— come in, you four at the door. Sit in these last chairs here." The four strangers join the circle, then the doctor continues, "I am Dr. Silver and this is Nurse Goode. We are going to begin Group Therapy for Singles and Couples Using Unconventional, Existential Methods. Welcome to you all. First, we'll split you into two groups based on your initial private therapy session when you arrived here yesterday. You've all been here since yesterday and have had a few hours to adjust and relax."

Nurse Goode switches folders from her hand and the desk and nods. She hands Dr. Silver a folder and points to a few people, "It was right, Doctor."

Dr. Silver points to half of the large group, "That may be perfect enough, Nurse. My friends, we need the eight of you to go to that side of the room and both groups will make their own circle."

The eight individuals go to the other side of the room as two circles form. Calvin and the three folks who walked in with him sit among four strangers. Another doctor, carrying another black box, and a nurse enter the other side of the room while a partition divides the room in two. The doctor and nurse squeeze into the circle with their chairs, next to each other.

The nurse sits down, "Is everyone settled?" The patients express various approvals, without color.

Dr. Silver doesn't waste time, "Okay, we have eight of you together now. You all have different lives and issues, but what you'll learn with us here is to not only overcome your adversities but learn to thrive in any environment. Maybe even ascend to levels you never dreamed possible." The people look at each other, and smirks of hope spread a bit. "I want to first talk about your health problems and issues. Well, the ones that you are aware of and will admit to us about. Nurse, who is first?"

"Belle Cantrell, Dr. Silver. Can add a thought?" The doctor nods to her. She continues, "I want to add that we may be strangers now in this moment, yet your individual truth of suffering should be labeled, discussed, faced, and referred to for future knowledge. Our journey together will prove of how little we should be afraid when in this company."

Dr. Silver first smiles at the nurse, "Excellent, Nurse... Belle, tell us what ails you, what is your relationship status if you want, and what bothers you," Dr. Silver points to a brunette woman, of great beauty in her late 20's, who projects a strong yet gentle energy. Her wavy hair and leopard-framed glasses both add to her sweet vibe.

"How y'all doin'? I have Crohn's Disease with Acid Reflux and am single out of choice. What bothers me? When people put others down to feel good about themselves, if I'm to be honest."

"Thank you, Belle. Your physical diseases also cause much psychological distress, which is nothing to ignore. Your other comment shows your true character, which is impressive... Calvin Wayne, what is your pain in this existence?" Dr. Silver asks the man with the spin-fidgeter.

"I suffer from Schizo-Affective Disorder, which is bipolar with aspects of schizophrenia, like hearing sounds and occasional hallucinations. I also have Severe Anxiety and Memory Problems, due to my use of Cannabis, to treat the Anxiety and bipolar symptoms. This toy here helps me focus and calm down," Calvin holds up the spin-fidgeter. "I have been divorced for about six years now. I'm not interested in flings because I'm the type that needs a woman's deepest understanding and compassion. And the only thing that bothers me is mind games. Whatever the reason, I don't care."

"You suffer a disease of the mind, Calvin, and nothing makes life harder than your mind giving you difficulties. I'll ask Brian Harper to go next..." Dr. Silver points to a middle-aged man of average height and hefty build, who seems hesitant. Hesitant, but also calm. He is young looking for a man his age, and his hands are strong and capable, yet perfectly manicured.

Brian's deep voice gets their attention, "I don't know if I feel like sharing my pains with strangers yet."

"I know it's difficult, Brian. We all have diseases and problems that we must contend with and the biggest issue I see everywhere is people who don't share that with each other. When you share what ails you, some of the burden lifts that part where you only think from within the problem. A new perspective frees you up a bit. And sometimes it can explain a certain restriction that holds you back."

"Okay. I, uh, lost my wife, Danielle, almost two years ago. I can't get over her death, which was a sudden cancer that didn't give us a chance to really say goodbye. I also lost all four grandparents, both my parents, my uncle, my Best Friend from childhood to suicide, and four Dogs over the course of 15 years." Brian rubs his forehead. "I have a certain pair of embarrassing health issues, but whatever. I have Urinary Problems and Nocturia, which is getting up in the middle of the night to urinate. They both kind of go together... I guess what bothers me is when some foreigner comes into my town and takes up causes against mine and my forefathers' traditions. Not a fan of outsiders in general. I wouldn't cause them harm, but I might keep my distance. I'd do anything for my fellow townsfolk, though."

"Thank you, Brian. That is a lot of loss— so much to create isolation. I'm glad you're here. Outsiders can resemble townsfolk, though, can't they?" Dr. Silver asks him.

"Maybe, sometimes," Brian opens to the question as Calvin spins his gadget.

"Looks are deceiving because we all put on our best out there to be seen as such. I hope you learn to open your mind up to the greater existence we all share," The doctor says as he looks at his list. "Next, Anna Foster," Dr. Silver points to a woman in her mid to late 30's with blonde hair. She trembles a bit and looks around without judging.

Anna speaks up in her Midwestern American accent, "I kind of don't want to share because it's such a deep pain and it has affected my trust in other people."

"We're all in this life thing together. If you share openly, you can discover how much power you have over these issues." Dr. Silver smiles at Anna.

"Alright, I'm Anna. I have been the victim of Narcissistic Abuse in two personal relationships. Because of jealousy, anger, and manipulation in relationships, I struggle with trust, as I said. I also have PTSD from a couple traumas in my childhood that seem to echo today. It's damaged me deep inside, beyond my thoughts and emotions. What bothers me, besides jealousy, is people who don't follow a holy path, but instead choose to torment and damage other people. Oh, and I have Varicose Veins, but they aren't anything but ugly right now. Should probably have them checked eventually."

"Wow, Anna. Thank you for trusting all of us in this group. I hope we are welcoming and comforting enough company for you, but we'll have to develop that as a group. Next is..."

Calvin sees a flicker in the light atop the black box and moves his head— *what is wrong with that light?* He looks around at other people of various races, and one of the people he didn't hear from yet, who sits tight with another patient, flickers. And then both flicker. "Dr. Silver?"

"Yes, Calvin?"

"Why did I see those two people over there flicker?" Calvin spins his gadget to drown any stray thoughts.

"Calvin, I don't see it. Maybe only you can see it?" Dr. Silver looks around and no one flickers. He turns to the fifth patient and Calvin sees the light, atop the box, distorting another patient. "Uh, where were we?"

He shakes his head and squints. Calvin doesn't believe the doctor, which makes him begin to breathe heavily and blink his eyes. He looks at the box and fidgets with his spin-fidgeter. He gets it up to a good speed, which helps bring him back down.

The entire group looks at him in his focus... It slips! He jumps to catch the spin-fidgeter, but fumbles it and bumps into the box, which nicks the light...

CLICK-HUM-POP! The light on the box goes off and each person loses their digital camouflage to reveal the same three other Humans and three pairs of different alien races. Calvin grabs the spin-fidgeter off the ground, puts it in his pocket, and returns with his seat as he joins in the collective shock...

"AAGH!" Everyone screams and looks around the circle. Calvin sees two pairs of different aliens seated— one pair is short with horns, and the other, a bronze-skinned ornate pair. Dr. Silver and Nurse Goode are the third alien species! The patients are all overcome as they look around at each other.

"Oh my God! Oh my God!" Anna is overcome.

"Wow, I must be dreaming," Brian looks at the non-human people.

The doctor and nurse have silver skin, four eyes and fangs, and stand around six feet six. Dr. Silver has a crested skull and the nurse, a smooth one. He holds up his hands, "Everyone please keep calm, we brought you all together for a very good reason. If it helps, you all come from the same universe."

"Not really," Brian stares around. "Calvin, you're black?"

Calvin chuckles, "Actually, my father is Dutch German."

"I know this may be difficult, maybe more to some than others." Dr. Silver points to each group: "The first four people who spoke are known as Humans from Earth, these two are Zor-ahns from Zor-ah, and the two over there are Gurrs from the planet Gurrea. Nurse Goode and I are known as Ellagantce. That's a fancy sounding 'elegance'. Now, is everyone calm again?"

"The name is a little on the nose, isn't it, Dr. Silver?" Calvin looks at the doctor and the others and processes what he has seen.

"I was thinking the same thing, Calvin," Belle adds.

"Why, do I look scary or something? Oh, the chrome and silver. Yes, I am a doctor with a specialty in counseling. While I realize this is all highly unusual for all of you, I can assure you that this is all worth what we want to show you. Besides, we're all people, right? Let's continue introducing ourselves to each other... This is Allegga and Igbogga Goleeka. They are gilded Gurrs. Would you both like to continue the discussion?"

They are a graceful and beautiful species with bronze skin and ornaments to go with various gold and silver makeup. A tall and lean species who seem strong and agile. "Hello to you all. I am Allegga Goleeka, a Pansexual Gurr which means I like the two genders of our people plus another form of gender. Igbogga and I are both androgynous Gurrs who blend the lines of beauty of our sexes, which is our choice. Our people are fluid and accepting, so I rarely feel out of place. I am frustrated by waste, which I too contribute to, but don't know how to do better."

Igbogga goes next, "Hi, hi. I'm Igbogga Goleeka. I suffer from Sexsomnia, a disorder where I wake in the middle of the night and attempt to engage in sexual activities. Since I am usually unconscious during the episodes, I wake in shock and embarrassment. Lack of support bothers me, but I get plenty from Allegga. Recently, I learned it is brought on by stress. Oh, I also get these weird cysts that must be removed or they just grow."

"Stress can exacerbate many illnesses and adversities. Fantastic, that takes a lot of courage to share, Allegga and Igbogga. All of you." Dr. Silver points to the last two people, "And, here we have the Zor-ahns, Zyus-Pahl and his wife Whee-Pahl. What is your story?"

These two people have horns that blend into a strong brow, like a ram, which shields a kind and almost innocent face. Zyus-Pahl, the male, is a bit bigger at about five feet tall. They look at each other often.

"I am Zyus-Pahl, and ready to step in front of my wife to protect her, so be warned. I deal with a Bulging Disk on my lower back and Dry Skin. Dry skin is such a nuisance, and when my skin splits, what a sting! And when my back goes out, oh wow, I must lie in bed, on my back, for days. Hmm, and I don't like anyone who threatens or disrespects me or my loving wife." He looks at Brian, "Like you, Brian, maybe we're not so thrilled with you either... In our people's ways, only the married couple say our names without the last name. I hope you all respect that. Whee, you're next."

"I have Bilateral Carpal Tunnel Syndrome and found out it is from the housework I do, plus, I write our town's stories down for future generations. Those things tire out my hands and wrists. I don't like it when Zyus gets upset, especially when someone calls me Whee without the 'Pahl'!" She adds in a soft way, "I also have sensitive skin."

Dr. Silver responds, "Thank you, Zyus-Pahl and Whee-Pahl. That was excellent everyone. Any comments or questions before we continue?"

"I have a question. How do all of you have the same diseases we Humans get?" Calvin asks the doctor.

"We all share the same basic structure of a complex organism, and diseases vary only in genetic code and the specific treatment needed. We all have different names for diseases in our own languages, but they usually translate. If it doesn't, you will hear the closest thing."

"Is that why we all speak English?" Anna asks him.

"The earpieces we all are wearing is an advanced technology with a translator which also utilizes powerful intelligence to make all our speech line up perfectly. We all hear our own languages."

Brian looks around and shows disgust, "So many aliens, this is insane. I don't think I want to be here anymore."

"Do you have an issue because they look different? You are an alien to them as well, after all," Dr. Silver argues.

"We're all people, in some way, but this is deceitful." Brian looks at Calvin and the aliens.

"Give him time, Dr. Silver," Calvin offers some advice. "I must say, it *is* nice to meet people from another planet."

"It's nice to meet you too, Calvin," Zyus-Pahl replies.

"Yes, nice to meet you and all of you. Yes," Allegga smiles in the comfort of their partner, while Belle and Anna smile at the majority rule.

"You can leave if you wish, Brian, but I think we can help you get to a place where you feel the same love for the rest of all life as you do your townsfolk. I'm glad you interfered with the black box and its use of illusion, Calvin."

"Interesting," Zyus-Pahl adds.

Nurse Goode smiles, "Now, we can officially begin the program, Doctor."

"Yes Nurse. Now, we're going to start a grand adventure through the Dimensions of Existence. All of us! Let's all sit back in our chairs," Dr. Silver instructs them...

The room converts and manipulates to fold down into an enclosed, round vehicle. All chairs become pods with control consoles, and a shared space inside. A clear canopy appears over them to become a sort of vehicle.

The black box makes a shuffling noise and rounds out into a sphere. Two legs stand it up, and then two arms reach out. A rudimentary, smiling face animates the sphere like an old kids' toy with peg lights.

"Ah, this is SOO, the Sentient Omnipresent Orb. SOO can tell you anything about anything from anywhere and anytime. SOO has all information fathomable. She will also enable us to travel anywhere imaginable. Say hi, SOO."

"Hi friends! I am SOO. Any questions?" SOO's delivery is dry and quick. A couple smiles emerge.

"See, that's why we love SOO. Moving on, this thing with the pods we are in right now is called the Instantly Adaptable Vehicle, or the IAV. The IAV can travel in any known universe and endure any known element, atmosphere, or force laid upon it. Any propulsion necessary is available to navigate the cool places. As you can see, the clear canopy lets us all see above the waist for 360 degrees."

"This is so far beyond what I was thinking when I saw that flicker. I thought we were in 'Group Therapy'?" Calvin smirks.

"Yeah, I mean, what is going on here? What kind of health facility is this?" Anna struggles to digest the situation.

"Calvin, Anna, everyone, I assure you, we are about to go beyond this realm to find great health and well-being. Does anyone wish to leave the group?" Dr. Silver asks them.

"I think I'll stay, Dr. Silver," Brian's mind opens. No one else makes a sound as Anna thinks it over.

"Glad to hear. You each have an input terminal for food and drink preferences that will be created instantly for you whenever you are hungry. Water is available to you from the fountain in each pod. As for the cabins below, all sleeping and bathing is together for the two couples and single for the rest, but totally adaptable. You can go below by keeping your hands and arms inside your seat and then step on the wide set pedals. It is all housed in this vessel. And your belongings have been sent to your cabins below."

"Good, because I have to go right now," Belle says as her pod closes above her descent. Zyus-Pahl and Whee-Pahl do the same. Calvin uses his input terminal to make a steak and baked potato.

"Okay, I guess this is a good time for sleep, food, potty, and a shower," Dr. Silver sits back in his chair as Nurse Goode shrugs.

As a couple of the others descend below, the IAV shrinks into a small ray of light, then disappears into a section of a subatomic particle. As they traverse the surfaces of other universes, they slip into one deep blue bubble through a tiny blip...

Chapter 2: Aquaverse

Blue. Shades of heavy blue to baby blue. Volumes are irrelevant in this universe encased in water, where sentient life seeks improbable survival amidst the great beings that swim and glide along massive gravitational forces. The warmth of nearby rock worlds and simmer stars shield the vulnerable from terror.

Small piercing noises interrupt a constant low, waving hum. Occasional currents shake all that stir, within the vicinity of the waves, and life has evolved around the common phenomenon. When two of these immense rollers collide, a small explosion resets the gushing space in bursting bubbles.

In a quiet part of water, a bubbly blast flashes the entry of the IAV. It shoots through a wave collision to some smooth liquid. They glide along, untouched, to a rock world with lights along its surface. Dr. Silver turns to them, "Now that we're all fed and rested, I want to welcome you to Aquaverse, the all-water universe where life is both terrestrial and celestial. Many universes have celestial beings too, but they differ so greatly. Later, we'll see how vast they are compared to us." The vessel clings to the planet's surface, then approaches a gateway of light. "SOO, how large is this galaxy?"

"Dr. Silver, Aquaverse is the size of the Milky Way galaxy, give or take a few hundred million stars, except the stars here simmer in the water. Most of them."

Allegga clears their throat and speaks up, "Did you say everyone in this IAV from the same universe or galaxy?"

"Yes, Allegga, Humans come from a galaxy they call the Milky Way

Galaxy. The Gurrs and Zor-ahns both come from the same galaxy but only the Gurrs have a name for it, due to advancement. They call it Great Spiral, I believe," Dr. Silver looks over at Igbogga and Allegga. They both nod.

Belle thinks to herself for a moment and asks, "Dr. Silver, what did you mean before when you said, 'The Dimensions of Existence?' What Dimensions?"

"Thank you for reminding me, Belle. Our journey began when we left our universe and skimmed through the 10th Dimension. It is more than those dimensions, but I'll start by giving a summary of them."

"Does this mean we'll see all of creation?" Calvin wonders about the trip.

"Well, the main grasp of it. But, to start with the tenth dimension, you must know the nine before it and that each universe created under all parameters will be housed within a ten-dimensional framework. So, access up dimensions from the base geometric and time combined livable third one you were all born in is always present."

"Do we need a notebook? I think a notebook might help," Anna adds.

"Sure. SOO- notebooks and pens for all, or you can use the tablets in your pod." A tray next to SOO opens and Nurse Goode passes out a couple notebooks. The Humans and Gurrs opt for a tablet. "Moving on? Okay, to make this easy for all, I will lay it out as simplistic as I can, so we can jump back if there are questions."

"Simple? Doc..." Calvin smirks.

"I'm glad you are in good spirits, Calvin. So, the first and second dimensions are a line and flat shape, respectively. The third dimension, where you're all from, exhibits present objects in linear time, and the fourth dimension is all of the third dimension at once, like a slice of each moment, crowded with all presence and awareness of that moment."

"This is a bit complicated for me, Dr. Silver. Any other way to put it?" Belle asks him.

"Hmm, yeah, I think I can. The fourth dimension is always the most difficult to explain and understand. How about, the fourth is such a dimension that you wouldn't get any privacy. An awareness that accesses all knowledge and thought and possible space for each passing moment. Or, you could say, from third to fourth is like going from all things within a huge universe to the life holding a universe while time passes. Is that clearer?" Dr. Silver looks around and sees the group's almost-nods. "So, the fifth pairs with the sixth dimension, the seventh with the eighth dimension and the ninth with tenth dimension. The fifth dimension is access to the possible futures of a universe and the sixth is all possible futures of a universe. The seventh is access to possible pasts of a universe and the eighth dimension is all possible pasts or 'beginnings until now' of a universe."

"Mind blown, Doctor Dimension," Calvin jokes.

"Not done either. The ninth dimension has access to any conceivable type of universe, one at a time, and the tenth dimension is not just access to all universes but the place where all universes are created. All and any possible known types of life, physics, and energy exist in all universes, almost infinitely."

"Are we in the ninth or tenth dimension? Aren't we just accessing this Aquaverse?" Brian wonders.

"We are in the ninth, but this is all primer for the tenth dimension, to come in a few days of exploration. There is much to learn, but I want you all to know that you can choose to stay in any universe we explore to live out your life. Remember that question for later, Mr. Harper."

"Okay, so we can go explore anything that ever was or that is to be?" Brian pushes for another answer.

"Indeed. I have much to teach all of you about what it means to not just live, but create bounty and love, through consideration," Dr. Silver says while looking outside the IAV at the light through the rocky surface. "I will now continue with the facts of Aquaverse. We are on a rock world, but these are not what they seem from the outside."

Igbogga jumps in, "Will we see some creature slither by or a great thing come out of that light?"

"This is why I love this job. Igbogga. Oodles of life exist inside these rock worlds. Let us commence." The IAV pulls up to the entrance. "As we pass through this full energy gate, you can all see a paradise of blue and yellow light, with green fields and blue lakes along the interior. This civilization along the interior lives with that miniature star in the center as its catalyst for evolution." A few flying craft zoom around with a small star in the center of a healthy society of people. Dr. Silver adds, "Oh, and another bit of proof we are viewing this dimension from a higher one is we can see them, but they cannot see us at this gate or anywhere we'll travel together. We *can* choose to interact with them though, by dropping down dimensions."

"Are ghosts just beings from higher dimensions? To be clear, are WE ghosts to them? Would they see us?" Zyus-Pahl asks while smiling.

"You have ghosts too?" Calvin is a bit spooked. "I guess that proves they exist."

"If one of them is in touch with a part of their self that doesn't deny such a truth, then yes, one could see us. When life forms dream, they can travel almost anywhere and will appear as a ghost," Dr. Silver answers the humanoid ram.

The people along the land inside are farmers and hunters, at an early stage of technological development, with beasts of burden to help plow the fields and bows and arrows that take down large beasts. A celebration, of sorts, takes place with two people in the center of a dancing crowd.

"Those people down there look like they're having fun and just like people on our world, Zor-ah."

The IAV cruises around the inside world while the passengers observe.

"They have a star inside this world?" Brian is in disbelief.

"Any interesting facts about this world, SOO?"

"This is the planet Pock, and the people are one race who have no need for domain or profit over another in their world because of their system of sharing food and supplies. Not only does this world have this tiny star, but it is of practical use. They can start fires, it keeps them warm against the unforgiving cold of the outside waters, and the inner surface keeps a pressure balance with the help of this star," SOO states to the group.

Brian looks confused and questions the place, "These physics don't make much sense to me."

"Yeah, weird physics. The people look like just another variation of people." Calvin continues, "They do look like they make a fair society."

"All Laws of Physics are relative to the universe. What is fair to you, Calvin?"

"Everyone gets enough when there IS enough," Calvin answers with frustration. "I've lived without. I've eaten little when the world had plenty. Not eating food that is available but out of my reach due to my lack of money made me angry. Then, my racing thoughts and emotions take over." He takes a deep breath and sips his water.

"You sound like a typical Woke Social Justice Warrior, Calvin," Brian snipes at him.

"You sound like an ignorant person calling me Woke. Life evolves and civilizations along with it, so when you say that I see a caveman wanting to stay in his cave and use his tools as is. The Social Justice Warrior is another stupid comment altogether, and I'll just respond with a simple quote from an obscure 21st century poet, 'from my shoes on me, you know not my pain, but as they tread on me, I see yours stained.'" Calvin wants to continue but does not.

Dr. Silver looks at Calvin, then to Brian, "Thank you for sharing those thoughts, Calvin. And, Brian, if you are so alone in your life now and you miss all those loved ones, why do you cast darkness on others? Is it their responsibility to bear the weight of your pain? Poverty is one of the worst situations for people in profit economies, where those in power care only for themselves, regardless of the type of government or empire. Many of these inner-world species, as they are called, were seeded by explorers whose limited technology marooned them and forced them to start over. They knew cooperation was the only way. SOO, what other threats does this world contend with during its float?"

"This world has not been taken by greed because the greatest threat to their existence is if a monstrous Gargan, one of the big whale creatures, breaks through an unguarded entry and drowns the entire people and all life here. It happens." SOO instructs them.

"Oh, is that all they have to worry about?" Belle widens her eyes as Calvin smiles at her. She blushes.

They zoom up to the center and see a star, with a diameter of about ten feet, that glows white yellow but without flares or other disturbances.

"As you can all see this little ball of fire is part of the physics and chemistry of the surroundings in that if it were to die, the planet would cave. These people are now discovering the waters outside and plan to build a structure on the outer surface that makes large water vessels. They plan for their survival," SOO tells the group.

The IAV coasts through the other side of the world and begins to pick up speed while a few of the travelers get drinks.

"Thank you, SOO. Let us move on to the next part of this beautiful blue universe. As we exit this planet, focus far away. You'll see great wiggles that inspire light and darkness within those faraway currents." Dr. Silver points ahead as the IAV moves at vomit speed, "We will shoot there. Ah, yes, these are the big fish of this galactic pond." The IAV slows to a stop and the travelers display nausea.

They approach a group of gargantuan beings that fight over a glowing gas giant. The beings, larger than planets, have long tails, and four legs. SOO chimes in, "This dim star of a mixture of gases is of pure delight to these huge beasts, which look like mammoth badgers to those on Earth or coilfuls to the Zor-ahns. But no fear of the dim stars running out as the center of this creation births many gas giants that ignite from within once they reach maturity."

"It would be fun if we could speak to one of them," Igbogga says with a smile.

"Ask if they can save a dim star for us to eat," Calvin says with a straight face.

"You want to speak with one of them? Okay," Dr. Silver says to Calvin, and drives the craft up to one of the monsters and as light flashes over them, startling the beast, "Hello, Gargan. Are you full after that star?" The IAV translates it into what sounds like horns blasting. The Gargan responds with loud noises and turns its back to the vessel with a blast of flatulence that washes by them.

They all smirk and giggle. "Mmm, gas. Tasty. I liked the world where everyone walked inside and upside down. Are there any inner worlds here, near these two giants?" Calvin wonders.

"Maybe a couple but they are more like outposts for larger and older civilizations."

"Hey, how did they walk along that surface inside?" Belle joins him in the question.

"The inside surface is ALL bottom. Or is that too easy?" Dr. Silver smirks through his fangs.

"Are there any other types of intelligent life here in this universe? Or is it just whales and ceiling walking farmers? I mean different species." Brian asks the doctor.

"There are a few different species, but they may all have still evolved from one species many, many eras ago. There are different levels of development in the inside worlds. Do you want to see the most advanced one?" Dr. Silver offers.

"Yeah," is the basic answer that is given among the ones with an opinion.

"Here we go." The craft spins around and shoots in an instant to arrive at a larger world connected to two smaller worlds through some sort of construction. Next to each world are large water vessels docked at considerable stations. Dr. Silver goes on, "Ah, we have a people who have traveled their universe and may feel like the universe is small now. Too bad if they feel boredom, because they have enough to eat and no one feels the need to profit from one another."

"This is cool. They know how to scuba dive, looks like," Calvin adds as he sees the divers fixing the water vessels.

"These people would love our huge, empty universe, huh?" Belle asks Calvin.

"No doubt," Calvin answers with confidence.

They fly through the intricate constructions of the people, connected by tunnels and safety stations. One station extends to an empty area of water, with a view to the center of the universe.

People walk through the tunnels, protected by advanced design, from one world to another. "Let's look inside the largest world here, where they are well beyond the planet Pock. SOO, any knowledge for us here?"

The IAV slips through the surface to reveal a vast interior with a decent star inside. SOO answers him, "Yes, buildings reach almost halfway towards the star which has allowed them to build a Star Feed, or as Humans have called it, a Dyson Sphere. It connects to the top of the buildings and provides endless electricity. With the worlds all enclosed in water, electricity is a sacred thing, and electricians are the most celebrated here. As much as explorers anyway."

Dr. Silver looks around and reaches to the panel, "Thank you, SOO. Any thoughts on how it relates to our illnesses and problems?"

"Everything is better when wet?" Brian says with a smirk.

Calvin adds, "You can be free in a world without greed," Calvin says without emotion.

"Yes, Calvin. There is truth to that." Dr. Silver nods.

"That giant water badger let out a big fart," Anna jokes. "I don't know if that will ever not be funny."

"I must agree, Anna. Alright, everyone. I feel like we are good with this Aquaverse for now. Just so you all know, you can each stay in any universe you wish to live out your life, though I realize no one will stay here. And I would encourage you all to remain with the group for the entire tour. Next, we will travel to the Black Hole Universe."

The Instantly Adaptable Vehicle shoots to the edge of the galactic universe and vanishes into a light blue water molecule, leaving a trail of bubbles...

Chapter 3: Black Hole Universe

Fiery light from the accretion disks, and the empty darkness behind it, gridlock the outer limits of this universe. Great stellar formations of star-baring celestial engines shield the inner cluster of galaxies from the ball bearing border of black holes. Occasional bursts blast from the black holes to slice through the arms of the formations, producing trails of sparkling dust.

The stars, including red dwarfs and neutrons, travel inward to the center of the universe to help create life, but only if too heavy for the gravitational grab of the great Singularities. Dusted colors bloom and swirl this network of stars, which hide the galaxies inside, from certain destruction.

In a small blip, the IAV and its crew enter the universe between two black holes and zoom by a few hundred stars in various stages of life. The vessel moves without interference from this place of fear.

Dr. Silver speaks up, "Welcome, everyone, to the Black Hole Universe. As you can see, the black holes are huge and they completely border this slightly elliptical universe, swallowing rogue stars in the process. There are more, smaller black holes in the centers of the few galaxies in the middle of the universe, called the High-Light Zone, which we'll see in a moment."

Belle's hatch opens and she returns up to her seat. She gets comfortable then downs the water on her console. "Did I miss anything?"

"We are in the Black Hole Universe. There're black holes on the outside, with stars surrounding the galaxies in the middle," Calvin summarizes for her with a smile at the end. He looks at Dr. Silver and gets an approving nod.

The IAV goes through the gases and young stars into the view of the small collection of galaxies that rotate around each other to provide stability. Zyus-Pahl and Whee-Pahl grab each other in awe.

"We're now passing through that little bit of chaos for the gases and sparks where stars come into being. This creates a brightly illuminated cloud for the galaxies from the black holes that surround everything."

"Can we travel through a black hole?" Brian suggests.

"Actually, why not? Let's check one out," Dr. Silver turns the craft around and they shoot to a singularity. They reach one black hole that emits a burst of light and fire in a straight shot. "There is what is called a 'random expulsion' or as Humans call it, a 'Quasi Periodic Eruption'. I love to watch them."

The IAV quickly crosses its accretion disk then the event horizon. The IAV's inside lights provide a decent glow in the surrounding darkness. "Look over there- another little star becomes a memory." The star he speaks of flashes and spreads around the outside, flashing yellow and orange lights along the threshold.

"This is beyond my imagination," Brian's jaw hangs.

As they approach the center inside, Dr. Silver speaks, "Here is the Singularity, a relatively small mass compared to the size of the entire flaming eight ball." The center in question spins and changes shapes as it barely glows. They observe for a moment then exit the other side of the black hole. "Anyone have any questions?"

"Do black holes that eat smaller stars lose more mass?" Calvin smirks at the doctor.

"I'm not sure, Calvin," Dr. Silver answers, then sees Nurse Goode with a grin. "Oh, I get it. Good one, Calvin."

The IAV shoots from the edges of the universe, through the gases and stars, to the High-Light Zone, which emits a homely aura.

"That was some bland diet humor, Calvin," Brian says to him.

"Moving on..." Dr. Silver takes a breath.

Zyus-Pahl speaks up, "So, there's life in these galaxies?"

"Yes, there is life. Lots of life. We like to show how life exists, endures, and exceeds."

"Exceeds how?" Anna speaks up.

"As in, a continuous evolution. Anna, we'll see in a minute that this species can travel through time. SOO, what are the two types of time travel?"

SOO smiles and answers, "Time travel within any given universe can be accomplished by two different methods. First, an individual may meditate and resonate within their atomic makeup to see beyond the moment in which they exist. The second and more popular way, because it doesn't require any type of painful or rightful path of enlightenment, is by means of technology."

"Thank you, SOO. How about some facts about this universe, guarded by its black holes."

SOO complies, "Yes, Dr. Silver, there are eleven advanced species within the eight galaxies of this universe. They do not interfere with each other except on occasion, unless you are referring to the cluster of four species who cooperate in one galaxy together. One species rules a galaxy alone, but a new, more aggressive species is close to discovering faster than light travel and instant manufacturing to challenge them. Let's hope they make peace instead."

"Uh, what is 'instant manufacturing'?" Brian asks the doctor.

Dr. Silver responds, "This IAV has it. Instant manufacturing is the technology that can make your favorite food or drink in a second by reorganizing atoms and putting them together so even your turkey gravy tastes good, and I can go full glutton on Earth whale without the guilt of killing an endangered species, which pleases Nurse Goode."

"Thank you, Dr. Silver," Nurse Goode smirks.

"Of course! Now, let's cruise closer to this one planet." Dr. Silver says as the vessel enters a galaxy and zooms in close to a star system. They circle a green and blue and gray planet.

SOO speaks up, "Here is a planet where the dominant species can travel through time. With all rules of time travel, one can travel in time but CANNOT touch or affect anyone or anything in the past that could change the makeup of their existence. It would undo the time altering journey in time, which would keep the past as is. So, instead a traveler can, at most, appear as a ghost, as previously discussed. Meddling in the future is fine because they're already part of creating their future. Educate patients about risks of Supers."

Dr. Silver steers the craft back out to the edge of the High-Light Zone. He adds, "It's kind of written in the rules, so they can have great fun and do things like learn each other's money codes and all kinds of sketchy things but nothing to collapse this wild universe. It is fun to watch, though."

Calvin thinks for a moment and asks, "Dr. Silver, are there any threats to us in the tenth dimension? And what are 'Supers'?"

"Calvin, yes, I'm afraid there are Super Beings that pose a threat to any of us that exceed specific limits. It is possible to outrun them, but hopefully we won't have to. Let's just avoid them. We could see one of these Super Beings in the next few universes, called 'The Lost'."

"Sounds mysterious," Belle wonders aloud.

Dr. Silver looks around at everyone, "It is said, 'Beware, you will pay the cost, if you tempt the Lost.' The Lost is a Super Being who hunts down those who interfere or influence a developing species or otherwise taint the natural evolution of that species."

"Any chance that thing over there is what you're referring to?" Calvin asks the silver doctor, who looks to his right to see a giant spectre watching spacemen in this universe's few galaxies. The Super Being has the appearance of a glowing ballerina, who stands 200 feet tall. The crew can't believe their eyes as they glance at them for just a moment, then look back and it shoots into one of the galaxies.

"Whoa. Is that another one?" Anna asks as they move to another view of the galaxies and find another Lost. "How did they come into being?"

"Wow, that is another one. The Lost were once living beings, who come from many worlds where injustice lives on. SOO, can you tell us how these Supers came about?"

SOO smiles and looks side to side, "These Lost are chosen for their unique sense of right and wrong, by beings known as the Collection. Chosen for their willingness to preserve innocence, they can appear in multiple star systems at once."

"Thank you, SOO. Nurse Goode, are everyone's vitals normal?" The doctor asks her.

"Yes, maybe Anna has a higher heart rate than normal, but she should be fine."

Anna responds to the cardiology talk, "Yeah, when we leave this crazy place. I'm getting scared about all of this. You sure this is safe for us?"

"We'll be gone in a few moments, but I was hoping to finish about the Super Beings and Demons. Any chance you'd be okay with that?

You can go down into your private rest area and relax on your own."

Anna lightens up, "I'll do that, thanks." She hits her pedals and drops below the closing hatch.

"I want to continue by telling you about two more Supers or Demons- Aurfuud and The Great Void."

Belle interrupts him, "Wait, now we have Demons?"

"We do, Belle, but we will stay safe as long as we adhere to my directions. SOO, can you enlighten us about Aurfuud and The Great Void, please?" Dr. Silver pets SOO lightly.

SOO smiles, "Oh, that's nice. Thank you, doctor. Yes, well, demon is just a name for something greater than normal life. First is Aurfuud, the Demon of Infinite Faces who dismantles inter-dimensional beings who abuse the dimensional balance of their existence, or those who inflict abuse on any between-life spirit. If Aurfuud wasn't around, a single rogue being under the control of Darkness could topple all of existence. An individual may be changed into something great or even unbearable. He's called a Demon but serves a purpose."

"That sounds like fun, I hope you don't get us in trouble, Dr. Silver," Allegga says to the host.

"You will all find that it is your own decisions that have the greatest impact on your lives. You can truly go far if you follow all the vital rules and are considerate of the space all life forms require to exist. SOO, were you still instructing us about the Supers?"

"Yes, thank you." SOO gives a robotic impression of an exhale, "Darkness, or The Great Void, is what it sounds like, and the best advice is to always reserve Hope within yourself for your Self. An echoing emptiness beyond measure is one path to that place."

"That is some vital wisdom and knowledge for my mental well-being, Doc. Thank you," Calvin smiles and nods.

Dr. Silver gives him his version of thumbs up and continues, "Nurse, please send my commentary on Aurfuud and The Great Void to Anna's tablet. I'll call Anna back now." He hits a few buttons on his tablet.

"Are we going to travel to see the people of the advanced world? It *is* on the itinerary," Nurse Goode informs the doctor as Anna returns to the group.

"Ah, yes. Let's take a quick look at the Human-like people on this world to see that they have developed teleportation, by spaceship."

The star system has a good collection of rocky worlds, many of which are inhabited by space settlers. Ships and crafts and structures show people who live off their stars. The IAV shoots to a planet and into its atmosphere, filled with a shading pink-yellow sunlight from two stars— a red one and a yellow one.

It is a world with a flat landscape of fields and forests, though there are a few mountain ranges spread out, and small cities that don't look overpopulated. The surface flora is green, blue, and orange. Organized flight traffic doesn't crowd the sky as the streets of the city express a celebration in colored decorations.

They land softly on the outskirts of a small town without interrupting the planet's people, who all run many kinds of machines. There is not one person strained or compromised in any way.

"But look at how similar they are to you four from Earth. Maybe a bit bigger due to their native planet."

"They are all beautiful, Doctor. I mean, they are physical specimens, like Ancient Greek mythology beautiful. And, like eight feet tall."

"Indeed, Anna. They *are* beautiful. SOO, what is the planetary data of this world?"

SOO replies, "Planet Vessas, compared to Earth of the Milky Way Galaxy, has 72% of Earth's gravity, so the average Vessasian is eight feet four inches in Human measurement. A bit taller than the Ellagantce of Dr. Silver and Nurse Goode. The surface area is five times and the land mass eight times that of Earth, with zero pollution. The people only farm crops for what flora they eat and with which they adorn their surroundings. They do not hunt or kill other life forms but sample the animals' flesh to program their food creators. Since they explore their galaxy and make new homes on new worlds, they are not only highly adaptable but also explore without hesitation to expand their footprint."

"That's weirdly descriptive, SOO. Dr. Silver, can we see their beaches and snowy mountains?" Calvin asks.

"That's sounds beautiful, doesn't it Zy?" Whee-Pahl asks her man.

"Yes, let's see a beach. Do they have clear water and purple-pink sands?" Zyus-Pahl looks at Dr. Silver.

"Let's find out," Dr. Silver responds after a nod. They take off and zoom over a few cities to a coastline, then skim around on the water. "Looks more purple blue to me. We can get out of our IAV but stay within the visible energy bubble. You'll stay dry in the water and invisible to locals."

"This world is so pretty. Dr. Silver, how fast do we travel in this IAV?" Belle asks him.

"Relative to the universe, we can travel any distance NI. As in, Near Instant. We can cover an entire universe, regardless of size, in a matter of moments. We restrict the speed to alleviate sickness. Remember, we're not actually traveling inside the universes— we're surveying them from beyond. We can travel to any moment in the entirety of any universe, so we'll go to ones where the life can inspire good discussions."

"Near instant is fast enough for me," Belle smiles.

"Are we actually still at that inpatient facility where we first sat in these chairs?" Anna asks the doctor.

"No, that is in the 10th Dimension, and each hallway of the hospital we were in is attached to a different world. The hologram made you all think you were still home. We are not far from that moment and place. We can go back to that moment if anyone has regrets, but I think you may all like the sand."

The IAV lands on the fine, purple sand and rests at the edge of the water. A dome of light comes from the top of the craft and surrounds a large area. The door slides open and they exit onto the sand without moving a grain. Calvin walks into the water and soon submerges to watch fish swim by him. Belle trots into the water behind him.

"We're dry in the water. Weird stuff. Not quite laying out at the beach, huh?" Calvin asks Belle.

"Nah, but the colors are unlike Earth, like someone painted this place. The fish are a bit different, huh?" Belle asks Calvin with cute eyes.

"They are— that one is a weird shape." They see one type that has two heads split apart and curved around to its tail fin. "What evolutionary purpose could that serve?"

"Maybe they both like the taste of their own, ya know," Belle ponders.

"Or maybe they both wanted to turn their own way."

Anna, Igbogga, and Whee-Pahl walk into the water near Calvin and Belle. The others sit on the beach and look around at the beautiful world. Whee-Pahl stays only a minute or two before returning to her husband's side.

"What else is around here?" Belle squints.

Calvin suggests, "We can't leave the bubble, let's sit on the beach." The two flirters walk up the slope from the underwater display and sit down near three-inch waves that tap the sand in front of them. Dr. Silver and Nurse Goode eat and relax next to the IAV, while SOO hands them drinks and napkins.

"These people have amazing things, don't they, Honey?" Whee-Pahl asks her husband.

"Yeah, look at the flying things that zooms all around. I mean, we've been in this amazing IAV machine, but our home world is. This is incredible." Zyus-Pahl is in awe.

"This is similar to our world, maybe just as advanced," Allegga says as they look around at the other travelers. Igbogga rolls their eyes at their partner.

"Okay, all aboard the IAV! How did everyone like this universe and its uniqueness?" Dr. Silver says as they all return to the vessel.

"Wild place, really," Anna says as she keeps an eye outside while she sits down.

Calvin lets Belle enter first and they share a smile. He answers the doctor, "It was nice and easy here, but would prefer to touch the sand. Or snow. Next time, maybe?"

The rest follow them inside and take their seats. The door to the IAV closes and the energy bubble retracts back into the top of the craft.

"Yeah, and that water looked so warm," Belle adds.

"Next time, Calvin and Belle. It would be nice to get out in the real cold, clean air. I'm glad you all enjoyed it. Any reflections on your personal situation so far? Does this place remind of a certain part of what it's like to suffer?"

"Darkness is out there and my suffering keeps me anchored," Belle holds her stomach.

"How about that there's no escape from pain in any Existence?" Calvin says for certain.

"If you must stay in one place, you may grow and evolve beyond your wildest dreams. So, be patient anyway," Zyus-Pahl adds.

"Well said, all of you. You have expressed some wise words and I appreciate your thoughts. Here, there is no escape from illness or death or difference of being. It is a place of controlled reality, and you'll find it here, in the High-Light Zone," Dr. Silver goes quiet and drinks some water.

"Wait." Calvin smiles as though he is being pranked. They all take sips of their drinks.

"Now, we'll move on to the next part of tour, The Doorway Universe," Dr. Silver says to the group, now settled into their pods.

In part of a moment, the IAV zooms out to the edge of the galaxies and shoots through the stars, clouds, and black holes— BLIP!

Chapter 4: Doorway Universe

Shining perfection of varying proportions and destinations give each doorway its own possibilities for what they are and how they affect those who break their exact plane of transfer. Galaxies within giant clusters, full of stars, are segregated with this great maze of portals that completes a universe made for the curious observer.

A few galaxies collide with the beautiful, rectangular parallelograms, sometimes in galactic proportions, either to disappear into mystery or reappear in mirrored fashion somewhere inconvenient. Broken reflections chop and clutter this realm which demands caution.

Into a place near the outer edges of this expanse, a small hole welcomes the IAV to begin its tour. They fly near a chain of doorways, each revealing its own mystery: one shows random shapes that collide in turbulent fashion, and another shows animated trees and animals of odd, but adorable design singing and dancing.

As the craft continues to avoid the dangers, there is a large portal with no reflection before them. Once they come into full view of it, a smaller one with lines inside interacting, disappears into the larger doorway.

"Folks, I want to welcome you to the Doorway Universe. You will see many, many portals to go along with a good many galaxies. Life is abundant but they are aware of the giant and mysterious dangers of the skies. There are many types of portals in wild place. How many SOO?"

SOO quickly answers as it points to a certain one, "There are millions of them. That portal with lines, that disappeared a moment ago, is a two-dimensional doorway, which is nearly impossible to return from once you are there physically."

Dr. Silver jumps back in, "The doorways are kind of an unusual aspect considering the riskiness and randomness. We'll pass by the rest of these in deep space and cruise closer to the galaxies. I believe this universe is larger than the last one by good measure. SOO, any details about this universe?" Dr. Silver asks the sphere.

"Yes, Dr. Silver. The Doorway Universe has a network of portals, including the more basic dimensions, the first and the second. Others transport objects around the universe by the presence of sixth dimensional artificial intelligence to see all possible futures, so that exit points remain collision-free. There are over 15,000 intelligent species in 1280 galaxies, but few are developed enough to interfere with each other. Most of those 15,000 are industrial level civilizations, or beyond. War exists on some worlds not inhabited by the few dozen with advanced technology, and those few are familiar with the network of doorways."

"Thank you, SOO. Any questions as we look at these exciting things?" Dr. Silver asks the group.

"There are portals that can turn me into a line?" Zyus-Pahl looks at the doctor.

"That is correct, good sir."

Allegga smiles at Zyus-Pahl then asks the host, "Do you lose all consciousness?"

Dr. Silver thinks a moment, then answers, "I'm not sure, but interesting question. I don't want to find out."

"Are there any really destructive species that leave worlds worse off than how they were found?" Calvin questions them.

"SOO?" Dr. Silver passes the buck.

"There are several species in this universe who cannot stop their paths of great destruction. Often, a few will war with each other and take many lives, unnecessarily. This happens in many universes. When more competition becomes apparent without balanced leadership and wisdom to distribute resources fairly with compassion, fear of not enough takes over."

Calvin jumps in, "Or greed. It's a me over them."

"SOO sounds woke- like it's trying to change my beliefs about things. I didn't buy it. Earth does well with its system of Capitalism, and yeah, there may be some people who don't benefit from it, but I mean. I have done well, and I didn't get a fancy education. I mean, I have a degree, but I went to a community college that doesn't have sports teams. Many of my childhood friends, though, are either broke or begging me for money. They could all get up and pull themselves up by their bootstraps. I may have lived at home until I was in my early thirties, but I worked my butt off and did well."

"Brian, I'm glad you expressed that side of things. Anybody have a rebuttal?"

Calvin raises his hand and speaks up, "I think you may be full of soup, Brian. I mean, you think because you benefited from something, it's okay, even when someone tells you how badly it hurt them? Your friends need you and you ridicule them for not doing well? You're callous, dude. And it sounds like you were born on third base, so you should be grateful for what you've had in your cushy life, instead of judging others for not. I am sorry you have lost so many people in your life; it sounds like a tough row to hoe."

"I think I'll stop before I say something that Calvin really hates," Brian says with passive aggression.

"Piss off, Brian." Calvin steams and struggles to contain himself. He then explodes, "Screw this! Admit you are dead inside. All you are worth is the amount of money you have."

Brian smirks, "You are right about that, but don't lose your cool. Be an adult."

Calvin lets out a low, sarcastic laugh, then regains his composure and replies, "Dude, you are so lucky we are in this situation."

Dr. Silver holds up his hands, "Okay, that is where I call you off each other. This is one of the most contentious arguments from their planet, those two. Belle and Anna, any thoughts?" Dr. Silver points to the women.

Belle looks at Anna and answers first in her sweet, Southern accent, "Well, I am not sure if Anna agrees with me, but I like to take both sides for what they are and then bring them into reality. My mind's version of reality, that is, and I see that when people lose their regard for others' well-being, society seems to make less sense and people act more fearful."

Anna nods, "Yeah, I agree. People who are successful and have pulled up their bootstraps, as Brian said, should be grateful for what they have and pass on to others that good fortune."

Calvin follows Anna, "Yes, and that good fortune will make society richer in ways an individual's pampered life cannot."

"Why do you think it is okay to keep it all to yourself, Brian?" Zyus-Pahl asks him, but no answer from Mr. Harper.

Dr. Silver drives the IAV toward a herd of galaxies, which are somewhat isolated from the main flow of portals. They coast in towards one lonely portal.

Brian answers the Zor-ahn while withholding his temper and a strong desire to unload all emotions on him, "Well, Zyus-Pahl, If you saw the amount of entitled people who think they can lay around and have the government take care of them when they could be out working— I know there are jobs back home for everyone to succeed if they just put in the effort. Nothing comes easy, ya know. I think many people are just jealous," Brian argues.

Igbogga speaks up, "What good is your world if many people suffer in plain sight while you indulge? Our people succeed in all areas and people that don't win aren't brushed aside but are considered part of why anyone would win in the first place. You can't win alone."

"I would add that you can either make everyone else an enemy that you don't consider familiar, or you can open up to the common truth of life: we all feel bad when discarded and we all feel good when included," Allegga adds.

"Such disregard for you to bask in the glory at their expense is a fool's paradise, and I see why Calvin argues with you, Brian," Zyus-Pahl tells the apathetic man.

"Alright, I will turn this car around right now! Did I say that correctly, Humans? SOO, can you tell us about the species of this planet in the galaxy ahead, who use the portals to explore new galaxies?" Dr. Silver takes the lead back. There are a couple of smiles.

The IAV zooms into one arm of a spiral galaxy, whose stars are plentiful and full of life, to a giant star with a dense assortment of planets on staggered elliptical orbits. Ships and structures decorate this system with many scientific questions answered.

They arrive outside the atmosphere and descend while viewing different terrains everywhere. Beaches and cities, plains and fields of crops, and industrial zones with steam exhaust disappearing in puffs. Mountain ranges sit faraway from an apparent equator of sand. They zoom in to see many boats and gatherings on an island of castles. The craft slows down above the warm beaches where folks have fun in the water.

SOO replies, "Yes, here is the planet known— "

Dr. Silver jumps back in, "Actually, SOO, we don't need the names of the planets we visit, unless someone asks. What matters is the view and what there is to learn of how a species uses their technology to create or destroy. Please continue, SOO."

SOO stares at Dr. Silver for a moment, "Thank you, Doctor. Anyway, this planet is a touch larger, but its mass is like that of Earth, Gurrea, and Zor-ah. There are six moons in orbit to confuse the tides, and some have breathable atmospheres. It has a wide array of elements, common and rare, which has given people an exposure to science but not radiation, surprisingly. They have developed nuclear capabilities and other dangerous advancements on their moons, one of which has dense uranium growth. This helps keep their home world safe."

"Dr. Silver, any possible way we can see the mountains here?" Belle asks Dr. Silver.

"We certainly can, Belle," the doctor answers.

The IAV takes off from its crawl and cruises past the parties and celebrations to communities of other more serious purposes, and then over many cities and industrial grids with clouds of steam. As they make their way over barren lands of sparse weeds and settled snow, the size and scale of the mountains give them all a moment of awe.

As they pass over the thick, settled snow and into falling flakes of white, Calvin has an idea, "Is there any way we can get out of this vehicle and touch the snow? I haven't seen snow in a few years, besides seeing it outside my window yesterday. I love snow."

"Me too. Can we, Dr. Silver?" Belle assists Calvin.

"Hmm. I can alter the bubble so we can all stand in the snow, but we still must remain inside it," Dr. Silver tells them.

Allegga takes a stab, "Yes, of course we will stay in the bubble. I want to stand in the snow."

"Allegga, well said," Dr. Silver warns them.

"Aw, come on, we'll stay next to the IAV. Just to touch the snow, Doc," Calvin tries to push his host.

"Oh, okay. Let's cruise to this spot over here," Dr. Silver tells the group. They find a plateau of untouched snow, where the IAV lands. "I am about to materialize us within the bubble, in this world and dimension."

The IAV descends dimensions in local, snowy winds that bounce off the canopy with a bustle. This startles Whee-Pahl, who reaches for the embrace of Zyus-Pahl before they exit the craft. Snow begins to gather atop the vessel, but it slides down the curves to the ground.

SOO speaks out, "All lifeforms that exit this vehicle must stay within the projection of the camouflage to remain out of sight of the local population. And The Lost."

A door opens and they walk out into the snow, within the tent shape of lights that form their border. Calvin gathers a handful of snow and packs it, then tosses it at an unsuspecting Belle's rear end.

"Hey!" She grabs some snow and tries to throw it back, but it tags Anna.

"Oh, that's it!" Anna gets a snowball and throws it, but it hits Allegga.

"Ooh, is this a snow fight?" Allegga asks. "We don't have snow on Gurrea, just occupied worlds with occasional rains or even constant downpours. We don't travel much, do we?" Allegga looks at Igbogga. Allegga packs some snow and throws it at Calvin, but he dodges it with a cocky laugh.

They all begin to toss loose snowballs at each other, a light they all share, except Brian. He sits down on a mat and holds some of the snow in his hands, taking a moment to enjoy some of it melting into warm water along the edges of his fingers. The doctor and nurse tend to the travel itinerary on their tablets.

"No, we like our theater shows in our esteemed city." Igbogga gets a snowball in the face from Whee-Pahl, who joins the fun. "Ooh, I'll get you!" It escalates into a war of snow.

Dr. Silver and Nurse Goode seem amused, and Nurse Goode leans over to him, "It looks fun, doesn't it, Doctor?" She smirks and opens her eyes, then grabs a ball of snow and pelts him before he can react.

"Well, now you've forced my hand!" Dr. Silver gives in and the snow flies as SOO smiles from inside the vessel.

Whee-Pahl tries to duck from a shot and slips. She slides off the plateau and out of the lighted zone! A few see her and hurry to the edge. Whee-Pahl sits on a small cliff, freezing. Zyus-Pahl panics, "We have to get my love, I'm going down there before it's too late!"

"Yes, someone must get her immediately!" The doctor warns them.

Without a thought, Calvin jumps down to the ledge, which is about eight feet down. Lights appear out in the distance. It's a group of flying machines from the population! "Baayu-agglle-way!" The language is garbled and foreign, and the two travelers know they must move at once.

"Put your arm around my neck, Whee-Pahl," Calvin commands her.

"Okay. Thank you, Calvin." She puts her arm around his neck, and he hoists her up to the accepting grasps of the others.

Zyus-Pahl overhears her and huffs, "Lift her up here!"

Belle looks up, "Oh no, up there— It's The Lost!" The great being zooms in from above, while the local people float, and watches Whee-Pahl disappear, then Calvin gets lifted by the others back into the bubble. They all rush back into the vessel, without an issue, and settle into their seats.

Dr. Silver gets them off the ground, and the IAV begins to reascend dimensions with some sparkling flashes. The Lost, now too late, swipes her hand at the IAV, then chases it. The native flying crafts stare at nothing and turn around.

All 10 travelers exhale simultaneously as the IAV makes distance from The Lost, which chases them out into the portal-filled cosmos. She lets out a roar when the chase becomes futile, then returns to scope local life again. They shoot to the edge of the universe where it all stays within their viewing perspective.

Dr. Silver looks around at everyone, "Well, that was fun, wouldn't you all agree? Now we all know why I stay away from some places." They just look at him. "Does anyone have a thought or two of how this place can be similar to your problems?"

Zyus-Pahl speaks first, "I think because there are so many doorways and dangers of that sort that it is like the many ways we can go wrong in life if not careful."

Allegga nods and adds, "I also feel like The Lost are similar to my unconscious mind keeping me from leaving life's path."

"I like that, both of you. Anyone else?"

Calvin adds, "I think when we experience things like what would have seemed impossible to most of us, it builds you up. I can see the possibilities."

Dr. Silver nods and smiles at him, "Excellent, Calvin." He then looks around, "Shall we move on? We will now go to the universe called Polar-Verse." Silence dominates the craft as he turns around to operate the vessel. Belle drops below. The others follow.

The IAV backs up to the edge of the universe and slips through a small hole in the fabric of space, as portals crash and envelop each other nearby…

Chapter 5: Polar-Verse

Beyond measure from any life form within, this massive expanse stretches between two great, eternal engines locked in a perpetual cycle of addition and subtraction. One end could swallow this existence itself, and the other would create it right back into being. Energy and matter leave the universe at one end while it comes into being at the other end as gas, a cycle that defies all reasonable thought.

Outpouring from the great birthing origin are the developing stages of a universe's evolution, from the thick collage of gases to the smaller galaxies to the larger ones growing farther apart as they become more massive. The wide belt of the universe retains a steady population of elder galaxies, where an occasional space egg spirals into the deadly maelstrom of the terrifying exit.

Many galaxies in the belt are physically balanced and move at speeds one would calculate in a universe of this nature. They sling shot each other to create a circular current of celestial creations— a dance which keeps each star's ice pocket guarded from the universe's processes. This makes them hospitable for life-bearing planets.

Stardust splashes the entry of the IAV, then disappears to reveal the natural light of this universe. "What a ride, huh?" Dr. Silver looks back and sees Belle, Calvin, and Anna return from their lower compartments. He continues, "Welcome to the Polar-Verse, everyone." They gaze upon the cycle from afar.

"This universe is larger than the others, so far. Right, Doctor?" Nurse Goode asks him.

"Yes, Nurse Goode. Let's let SOO tell us about this unusual place we are visiting."

SOO chimes in, "The Polar-Verse is bigger than the Doorway Universe, but the Polar-Verse is one of the most complex in all of Existence. It has a Big Bang at one end and a Big End at the other. You will never find a more turbulent place for matter and galaxies to develop and endure, yet they interact with each other's gravity to swirl throughout the considerable space. This comprises the whole design of the universe."

Calvin jumps in, "That sounds like the Black Hole Universe, which had a small group of galaxies in the middle. Just different outside, but a similar pocket."

"Good eye, Calvin. Yes, you will find that many universes share features and designs, but these two are pretty much the only ones with all its galaxies inside a pocket. All others spread it around more, don't worry," Dr. Silver nods at him.

"How many galaxies and advanced civilizations reside here?" Dr. Silver asks the sphere.

SOO responds quickly, "This universe has hundreds of thousands of galaxies and even more species that are considered at least moderately sophisticated. Life does not leave the confines of the wide belt because they soon realize that their ships cannot withstand the onslaught of heat, pressure, rock, and debris."

"What is a 'Big End'?" Belle asks with skepticism.

Dr. Silver answers, "The Big End here takes all the excess everything and recycles it under the surface of the universe until it reemerges from the Big Bang, which happens to be one constant 'Bang'."

"Yes, God, yes!" Belle jokes. Calvin is the only one to laugh as Anna withholds her chuckle.

"Dr. Silver, is this universe like ours other than the two ends?" Calvin asks him. "Does our universe still have a Big Bang end that continues to feed it, something crazy like that?"

"I don't think so, off the top of my head, but you guys had other rules that made things harder. For one, your universe has the harshest conditions in deep space: vast distances, harsh elements, and the strictest paradoxes intertwined in the discoverable laws. Mathematical rules stay consistent enough but mean nothing without the concepts of creation that unlock God's truth and love to all life."

"That may be too advanced for this group right now, Dr. Silver,"

Nurse Goode thinks aloud.

"Yes, perhaps. I want to show you all a world where many species live and thrive. It is an assembly of many planets who surpassed their individual apocalypse and gathered to create order and peace for all life within their combined rule. This world is a paradise, of sorts, and they share it in the celebration of their unity."

The IAV darts into the pocket and passes galaxy after galaxy. They scoot inside one toward a light blue world with lime green land and white sands. There are large, striking vessels and spaceships, which rest in docks. Spacemen fly about and disappear into an orb that sits in space near a populated moon.

Zyus-Pahl asks, "What is that orb?"

"That orb is a wormhole and they can travel anywhere in the known belt of the universe. They are the only ones here to have the capability of folding their dimension of space," Dr. Silver answers him.

"Fascinating," Brian says, almost to himself.

They float down to the surface, in haste, and circle some cities with varied styles and structures, but all royal or extravagant design. The ship coasts over some beaches and the stores that make it look like the 'shore'.

"Whoa, this is really pretty," Anna says. "I wonder if it's considered an intrusion to be among these people since we are less advanced. Is it okay?"

"You'd think, but very few living beings have ever known of this craft and where our travels can go, which is beyond their grasp. As they say, all things own a purpose." The doctor presses some buttons, and they land on a hill with a view to a town of white sands and clear waters. The people are only different than Humans by things like their growth of fur along their shoulders and heads. Some have big ears that seem reddened by the warm sun.

"Is all life basically the same?" Calvin wonders. "Is every advanced species two legs, two arms, and a head? Are there any other types?"

"That's the same?" Brian interjects. "Looks plenty different to me."

Dr. Silver replies, "Right on time, Brian. We show you similar life to yourselves. You might have obvious differences, but you're all types of people, or beings. I don't care what each of you looks like, it is always the content of the person's soul that deserves respect or can enable them to create."

"That's beautiful, Dr. Silver. Thank you for reaffirming that good exists out there," Anna's inner strength begins to grow as she begins. "You have a lot to learn, Brian. You seem loyal and kind. In your way, but you still seem to be stubborn in a way that keeps you from truly living. I can say that I have been in bad situations, and felt hopeless and hurt, but if you can break the cycle and escape, you have a chance to face your pain and learn from it. You may never spend another moment wallowing OR avoiding the trouble again."

"Maybe, Anna, but I just keep my head and forget about all that soft stuff. My Danielle always supported me as I made sure, we never went without enough plus some extra."

Dr. Silver adds, "Brian, I can promise you that when a person doesn't reflect and learn to show compassion to oneself and others in a healthy way, they will remain on the verge of or during despair. We could both stand in an empty field, but would you taste the wind, and hear shadows crawl by, while seeing forces of all kinds that keep you there?"

Nurse Goode jumps in, "Dr. Silver, I think we should focus on the planet here and let Brian come into his own as the trip happens."

"I am learning so much about random things, it is just so. I am very happy to be here!" Allegga blurts out.

"Allegga, you on something good? I want some. I think we've been here together long enough to share," Calvin jokes, drawing several grins.

Dr. Silver smiles at the group's exchange and continues, "You are right, Nurse. Brian, you are most definitely allowed to have your own views, and they will never be taken from you. But, let yourself grow emotionally. It only hurts at first. Open minds give way to great art within. Anyone else?"

"The only way to the true, genuine self is through pure honesty with yourself," Belle states with confidence. "My Daddy taught me that when I was first diagnosed with my Crohn's. I was only about 20 years old when I developed a stricture in my intestine that was thundering pain. I wouldn't wish it on my worst enemy or an evil stepmother. The only way to survive something like this is to be honest about what I can do and will do for my health."

Calvin watches Belle talk and he tears up with her talk of suffering. "Belle, I'm sorry you were tortured by your body like that. It must've been rough."

"It is awful, Calvin," Belle breaks down a little bit.

"Wow, thank you. Both of you," Dr. Silver smiles through his big fangs, then looks at his tablet. Nurse Goode and he make eye contact, then he continues, "I have received word from my superiors, who control The Lost, and we have been granted a beach day, for real this time."

Zyus-Pahl asks him, "I thought you just told us they wouldn't understand?"

"Apparently, these people are part of an intergalactic association of worlds who won't question our appearances. I will camouflage the IAV as a small space craft," Dr. Silver replies as he works the controls. The IAV transforms into a local spacecraft, reappears, and lands on an open plateau, near a serene coastal village.

"This is so cool!" Calvin is pumped for the occasion. "Any rules or regulations first?"

"Be polite and avoid interactions with others, but not in a weird way. We do not speak the language here, but you have your earpieces, so no big deal. They will translate your words so you can reply in their language. Once again, be polite. Keep all conversations within our group and go below to change into a swimsuit." They drop below for a moment. One by one, they return the canopy. "SOO, please let me know if there is an issue."

"You got it, Dr. Silver."

"Well, let's go then," Brian hammers them.

They get out of the IAV, which is one of many crafts perched in a hoard of plateaus around the base of a small mountain. A barrier of light swims over the ship and then dissipates.

Down the hill and towards the stores and the beach, the group is together but broken up: The Zor-ahns and Ellagantce walk together, the Humans walk in pairs ahead, and the Gurrs hold each other in the back as they gaze upon the natural beauty all around.

The way there is a hot, brown brick road, with homes on each side. All types of people pass by or commit their focus to their own yard or garden. The colors here are bright and blast around, but all seem connected to their inner peace.

All are within earshot of an inside voice on this peaceful day. "This is like a school trip when I was a child," Anna shares some nostalgia.

The other Humans nod with her.

"On Earth right now, we'd all be baking badly. I mean, it looks hot and scorching here, but it is this perfect balance of warmth and something else. Can't figure it out."

"This planet may have a lighter mass than you are used to, Belle. You may be able to jump far here, but I will need you to resist the temptation," Dr. Silver warns her.

"Fine. It feels good, though," Belle goes along with him.

As the travelers walk up the road, they spread out and keep to themselves. Calvin and Belle see a store selling goods for the beach, across the street. When they reach the store, the rest of the group looks at them.

Dr. Silver says, "Have fun and be cool."

Calvin says, "Hey, it's me, Doc." Then, he turns back to Belle, "Go in?"

Belle nods, "Sure, let's go. You do the talking, but don't get wild."

The group walks toward the dunes. Anna and Brian walk next to each other, and don't talk much.

Belle follows Calvin into the alien beach store where towels and boards cover the walls. Sunglasses of different styles and sizes are on racks and other doodads. Calvin leads them to a counter where a person with huge ears stands waiting for them.

"Hello, hello. Are you from a new world in the galaxy? I don't recognize either of you. I hope you enjoy this beautiful planet we call Glory."

"Uh, yes, we're from a new world and our people just joined the assembly. What does a body board cost here? Do you accept weird trades from off world?" Calvin asks the man.

"Oh, your people use money still. We supply for the common good of Glory, our world. All things are free, but do not waste that which you take and do not discard in public space. Do you want to take a board for fun and bring it back later? You can also find another beach lover to give it to."

"Thank you, sir. We'll take these two boards and these towels." They grab two towels and two boards from the walls. "Thank you and see you later." Calvin trades smiles with the man.

They exit the store and head to the beach. "Cool. So cool, Calvin," Belle smiles and gives a light smack to Calvin's shoulder. "We'll bring this stuff back. It's kind of a convenience."

"Or we can forget and leave them where we feel like." Calvin jokes but Belle is not amused by him. "Or we can give it back. Let's see first, okay?"

"Yeah, we'll see."

The rest of the group is gathered on a dune ahead. Brian and Anna notice Calvin and Belle come out of the store, then he looks back and throws up his hands. Anna laughs at him and drags him back to Calvin and Belle.

The four Humans come together, and Calvin is the first to speak, "Brian, everything is free here, so you can go in any store and grab what you want. The two main rules when obtaining goods is don't take more than you need and don't litter. Oh, and the guy doesn't look like a white guy from Earth so be cool."

"Whatever. Anna, want to get a body board?" Brian asks her.

"Sounds fun. I might want sunglasses if they have them. We'll see you guys on the beach."

Belle smiles and replies, "Sure thing. I'll be tanning." The foursome splits up into duos again.

Calvin and Belle go up to the beach and see a sparse crowd. Their group is gathered at a spot near the water and away from other people. The travelers are treated as townsfolk.

As they approach the group, Calvin runs into the water. He splashes around and does some strokes on his back, then says to the others, "This water is perfect."

"I may have to go check it out. I have a high tolerance for perfect things, like water and beaches," Zyus-Pahl jokes as he trots to the water and does a little dance as he tiptoes into the nice water. "Not bad. I may stay in here a minute." He dives in and swims for a moment but is startled by a large wave or something approaching.

A figure becomes apparent in the star's reflection of waves as a large man with scales and fins pierces the surface. He changes into a human looking man while Brian holds his board at the water's edge. The being who walks past Brian is about two times taller than the human.

Brian then turns around and returns to his towel, "No thanks, I'm comfortable out here."

"Sure. That guy scared you, didn't he?" Dr. Silver smirks. "How long does everyone want to stay here before we head back and have a barbecue at the IAV?"

Most shrug in response. Calvin answers, "Doc, this is nice. What do you think, Belle?"

"I like it here for now," she responds.

"Okay, let's stay for a minute and sunbathe. But, since I don't tan, I'll just chill."

The travelers are gathered on their small plateau with the IAV in spaceship form. Four play a lawn game while the rest watch.

SOO watches the group with a smile, "This is what everyone calls fun? I guess it's better than big game hunting."

The doctor brushes off SOO's comment by opening reflection, "Does anyone have any thoughts or feelings about our journey right now and a problem?"

Belle answers, "This place is extraordinary, but I didn't feel an impact regarding my health. It just seems like another place."

"The two ends of the universe are extremes like my mental illness, but there doesn't seem to be any real turmoil here. This is like the calm before the storm. I guess it doesn't always appear, but the storm usually hits hard right after this," Calvin seems easy.

"I kind of agree with you both. I wanted to bring you here as a break from the trip. We are in no real danger here as everyone is different and we all learned a good lesson in the portal universe."

Igbogga jumps in, "This place was really soothing, even though we didn't relax very long on the beach. I feel at ease, like some of the worries I had that I can no longer identify, have disappeared."

"Wow, that sounds significant, Igbogga," Dr. Silver smiles at them.

"I guess we're not really barbecuing anything since these people eat from a food maker. Can I have anything then? I'm not a fan of barbecue flavors. In the mood for a burger." Calvin asks the doctor.

"Then, have a burger. Anyone want to eat now? The machine is ready. We can eat then relax a bit before we go to the next universe."

"Wait, I just thought of something. Why are we allowed to interact with these people on this planet here, but not the people of the planet where we almost lost Whee-Pahl?" Calvin asks the doctor.

SOO answers instead, "Some planets and universes are restricted and must never encounter people like you, who travel and have knowledge beyond normal life. These people here have been taught that there are forms of life that travel beyond wherever any living thing can fathom. The snowy place was filled with people who would've thought we were all Gods of some type."

"Oh, that's it?" Calvin grins at Belle, who giggles.

"Calvin, you're a goof," She flirts with him. "Oh, and Calvin and Dr. Silver, I get the humor, but I still say it would have been just as fun to return that stuff."

All that is left on the hill is the small pile of towels and body boards. A man of the town walks by the small plateau and shakes his head. He climbs up and walks around the area, where small divots mystify him.

"Where in Glory's name did that mess come from? I have a minute to clean up. Good thing it won't bring *me* down."

Chapter 6: Universe of the Dueling Furies

Perpetual tension and pressure consume this place manifested from two opposing, intertwined energies who dictate the balance of life and time here. The farthest points, where a glowing orange entity originates at one end and a shadowy purple one engages from the other, provide local stargazers with questions their science cannot answer. Galaxies swirl and absorb dust from those points of wonder.

Planets orbit their suns and stars, which orbit their galactic centers, and get their influence from each side of the universe. Their mystery of creation and why they are that which they are, is a puzzle to all those caught in the chaos.

Amidst the turmoil of energy, a puff of orange and purple dust explodes to welcome the IAV into the universe. They coast to a stop in the middle of mixed dust, so they can watch the two opposing forces at work.

"Welcome to the Universe of the Dueling Furies. We call it that because no one in this universe knows why they have two sides which are so at odds with each other. The Furies are two Super Beings who were once mortal siblings caught in such a profound level of competition that they created chaos and death around them. So, they were condemned to exist as deities of this realm for eternity," Dr. Silver states with appreciation for the place. "SOO, any facts for us?"

"Yes, this universe has galaxies in the center, and there are over two million galaxies here. It is not only the destined place of these two eternal spirits but those that dwell on their worlds are here to experience the great suffering they created in other universes. Spirits from everywhere who committed great sins on others. No advanced civilizations exist here, and people scrape by with just enough food for everyone, everywhere. The opposing forces undo all potential scientific breakthroughs with fundamental subversion. Other universes provide a similar destination for outliers to the general benevolence that existence is meant to foster despite its sometimes violent and unlivable creations."

"This sounds like Hell to these life forms here. The whole place is quite disturbing to me, Dr. Silver," Calvin admits.

Dr. Silver replies to him, "It is a sort of Hell that must be endured until the sweet freedom death will afford. All spirits here are in a fight, hide, or flight mode. About your comment, would you like to explain why it disturbs you, Calvin?"

"This is a bipolar existence, and I could see it that no one can withstand the torment of ping ponging back and forth between the two great spirits. It looks like my madness here. I need a minute." Calvin shakes his head and shuts his eyes, then drops below.

Anna takes a moment as she watches Calvin disappear then asks, "Reincarnation is the truth, then?" Anna looks at Nurse Goode, who nods back. She thinks a moment, "Does that mean that Jesus could be alive now, where we come from, in our time and place?"

"Well, the subject of Jesus and reincarnation is a good one. SOO, can you tell us about deities and planetary divinity?" Dr. Silver turns toward the sphere with a personality.

Calvin rejoins them. Nurse Goode whispers to him, "We're discussing Jesus and reincarnation." Calvin nods.

"Glad you're back, Calvin," Belle says with a smile, and he returns one to the lady.

SOO senses the silence and explains, "Every single planet that has life, has a primary spirit that has an open psychic connection with the Deity of their universe. That Deity is directly connected to The One. Jesus was his name in that lifetime, as the living Primary Spirit of Earth. He or she has returned numerous times, in different situations, to ascend or remain in all social classes throughout the world. Many Primaries do this." SOO inhales and exhales, jokingly, and continues, "It is all like a lotus, but obviously more complicated. All mortal spirits, without damnation, can each live a normal life or watch as part of the Holy Spirit. When a planet loses all life from an extinction event, the spirits can wait until life returns, be reborn elsewhere, or rejoin The One if the world becomes too damaged for life to come back."

"Thank you, SOO. Any questions?" The male Ellagantce touches his chest and kisses his fingers, then he points up.

"Are there any people here worth observing, Doc?" Brian asks him.

"They are all mostly the same here— desperate and selfish. It is a barbaric sight," Dr. Silver says without emotion.

The IAV cruises towards the galaxies.

"It is important to know what our limits are and I know you may all find some challenges here to your mind and self, so hang in there," Dr. Silver cautions them.

"This universe looks a little like the Polar-Verse. Two poles with a population of galaxies inside. Not the same though," Brian wonders.

"It looks like it. There are many types and shapes of universes but there are common shapes that they can take on to become a workable universe. Sometimes the shape doesn't matter, and the universe will take a form on its own."

They travel into the middle of the galaxies and enter one with two spiral arms. "Doctor, I think we should show them the planet... This one." Nurse Goode points at her tablet as she shows it to Dr. Silver.

"Ah yes." They zoom to a planet in haste, which has orange and purple dust clouding its surface. They slow down to watch some people, who live in caves and huts. "This one here, has been so heavily worn by tired old motivations that the people here are despondent and lazy. SOO, anything else?" Most people appear to live in a fog, but an occasional fight breaks out. They don't exhibit much beyond this.

"They seem dull and without much spark," Calvin says.

Some ruins attract people. The buildings, empty and deteriorating, have faint lights within. Upon what seems like a major discovery, one of them runs out of a structure with a blue torch and proceeds to swing it at his fellow citizens, who flee in a panic.

"Terrible to watch," Allegga says and Igbogga nods in agreement.

"And that is because they came from such wealthy and extravagant lives, for the most part, that they don't connect to the depths of their new lives here. Tough place to raise a kid, as well," Dr. Silver informs them on the world. "Important note, all Existence from one being's perception to The One, or Humans refer to as God, Gurrs say All-One, and the Zor-ahns say, what is your word, Zyus-Pahl?"

Zyus-Pahl responds, "We call him Great Creator."

"Thank you, sir. As I was saying, it is symbiotic, in that we feed off the energies of our universes and Creators all the way to God or the One or Great Creator or All-One. Did you ever get happy out of nowhere? Sometimes, Thou wants you to be happy. Thou feed off of us in a way we shouldn't discuss out of humility for what we don't know yet."

"This universe is kind of boring once you get past the craziness. Are there any other places here so we can see something different?" Brian gets impatient.

"You want something different? I can show you some of a mystery to all of you, Dark Matter and Energy," Dr. Silver mentions.

"Definitely!" Calvin is happy then contains himself a bit.

"Dark Matter is a part of space exploration and discovery that require knowledge of beyond a being's own universe. You eight people now have that rare access. It is a basic building component, along with Dark Energy, to make universes."

"Why haven't we seen that yet?"

"It exists in different scales from universe to universe. There is a small bit here, which helps insulate the galaxies." Dr. Silver gets cut off by Calvin.

"Is this another pocket of galaxies, Doctor? I thought the other two were *it*. I thought this was a population of galaxies. Hmm?" Calvin gets wise with him and Belle giggles.

Dr. Silver laughs and replies, "This isn't really a pocket, though. It is millions of galaxies with some deep space to the poles. Galaxies do get swallowed up here. Okay, it's a big pocket." He earns a few laughs.

"What are the two, Dark Matter and Energy?" Brian asks him.

Dr. Silver answers, "They keep in place the celestial objects that help each Fury cast influence. The exciting part is that the Dark Matter and Dark Energy come directly from a higher dimension beyond our ten here. We will learn their purpose from a place you will better understand them."

"Wait, beyond our 10th Dimension? This is nuts," Brian interrupts.

SOO jumps in, "Yes, Brian. We will cover those higher dimensions toward the conclusion of our trip."

"Thank you, SOO. This place should prove to all of you that worlds still value benevolence, even if there is confusion. Your worlds all want to preserve life. This universe teaches you the consequences for the destruction of life and harmony," Dr. Silver shows satisfaction with the group's collective silence regarding this sad place. "Let's see some of that tricky stuff."

The IAV shoots through the pocket and out to the bright glow of orange light all around. There is mostly light, with relatively small shadows of violet that move like clouds in the sky. As they approach a shadow, it disappears. Then, the shadows become morphing shapes of deep and dark purple.

"Uh, is it changing?" Calvin asks. "I see a cube then a sphere."

"Yes, they never stay in one shape, sometimes flash and spin like a neutron star. Always the same deep purple, a color that is almost invisible out here if not for the glow. Dark Matter is like nothing else. It can be different from one universe to another."

Anna wonders, "You also mentioned Dark Energy."

"Ah, yes, Dark Energy isn't seen in this spectrum. Let us move back to the outskirts where we split the two Furies and the pocket is before us." Dr. Silver winks at Calvin and then works the controls.

"I think I get why you didn't like this place, Calvin. Does it bother you still? Do you feel aware of your mental problems?" Brian instigates a response from Calvin.

"Are you trying to start with me, Brian? Just stop, man," Calvin holds up his hand to Brian.

"Anything to feel uneasy and unstable," Brian tries to find more buttons.

"Shut up, Brian. What is your problem?" Belle defends Calvin. Anna looks turned off by Brian and turns away from him.

Nurse Goode intervenes, "Okay, let's look outside. We don't need arguments in this place. Just in case."

They zoom through the cosmos in a couple seconds and turn to see it all from a distance. Dr. Silver continues, "Now, the IAV will change the spectrum input from the canopy." A field of lights changes the view of the entire universe from inside the shell to a grayed-out system with two poles and a sprawling web of purple electricity that surrounds every galaxy.

"That's cool, Doc," Calvin smiles and the others join him. The sight of the two opposing forces surrounded by this wonder now brings in a lightness.

"Thank the lucky stars we don't live here or some of those other places. I thought ours was a cold and violent universe," Anna nods into a grateful prayer.

"You said it, Anna," Brian smiles at her.

"I guess The Lost never comes here since they aren't advanced enough to travel to other worlds in the first place, huh?" Allegga asks the doctor.

"That is correct. If a fortunate soul here was to atone for and face the inner turmoil, they may reach a level of enlightenment that allows for time travel. If they meddle in existence too much, they could meet the Demon of Infinite Faces, Aurfuud."

Dr. Silver changes the canopy view back to the colors of the rivaling sides and their galaxies within. Any hints of Dark Matter and Energy now blend into the ballet of chaos.

"Did this place evoke any strong emotions we should discuss?" Dr. Silver asks as he looks at Calvin.

Calvin nods and speaks up, "Yes, this was a tough one to watch, though the actual life here more represents my sadness and depression, my mania is not really seen. But the chaos is on point. It is kind of liberating to see something so massive look like it."

"One of the most difficult places to be sick is the mind. You will struggle until you fix your mind, no matter what."

Belle holds Calvin's hand and they smile.

"I think I have something to add about this universe," Anna speaks up and gets undivided attention. She continues, "I felt like this is a place full of many abusers, like those I knew, who now get to shake themselves of the guilt of past lives. Maybe some of these folks will learn to become helpful to others and do the little things that make a big difference."

"Wow, so real. And I loved that last part, Anna," Belle touches her shoulder.

"I admire your strength in seeing how someone similar to one who has hurt you can still atone and become a good person," Whee-Pahl smiles at her.

"Thank you, all of you. I am still struggling with closeness, but it helps that I can express this and have ears on my side. I feel a rush of relief, it's like my heart is feeling again," Anna breathes in and out with renewing energy.

"Well said, Anna. Thank you. This helped me, what you just said. It's nice to have a group to share these things with. No doubt," Calvin says.

"I am impressed with you all coming together like this. But, Brian, I want to see you be a positive part of this trip. I know you have been through the ringer, but you will find solace in the company of these fine people. It is no more apparent to me that you all are the right collection of people to help each other get soothed from the negative thoughts that can prevent us all from moving forward," Dr. Silver looks around at each of them.

"Thank you, Dr. Silver," Zyus-Pahl nods at the doctor.

"You are welcome, Mr. Zyus-Pahl. Any objections to going to the next universe?" He looks around at the group and finishes, "Alright, let's move on. We can stop for the night now, so we'll begin again in the next universe."

The IAV shoots around through a good puff of orange and purple powder...

Chapter 7: Triniverse

Spinning and rotating, these three realms dance with incredible motion, in unison, to an unknown entropy its life may or may not fear. The choreography displays the beauty of untouched nature hoping to be left to its pure design.

As each universe passes, the echo of similar galaxies and celestial formations gives way to a closer view of similar worlds and echoing space travelers. Similar but still different enough to make this place a fountain of wonder to outsiders.

Through a small rip in darkness, the IAV appears outside the spin of the mammoth arms. "Everyone back and awake?" They nodded. Some stretch, but all have a drink and some food. The doctor continues, "Great. I want to show you what we call the Triniverse. Here, there are three universes that move together in harmony to help alter basic physics for the sake of safer space exploration and time travel. The inhabitants of each universe are only aware of the one where they live. For just a moment, we'll sit outside. SOO, any facts about the three universes and the life within?"

"Yes, Dr. Silver. The three universes of Triniverse are perfectly balanced to keep physics simplified so early life could advance faster and explore space with minimal technology. Space is not harsh inside but is quite warm. One can put on a covered helmet of basic technology and traverse almost any reach of their universe. Another fun fact is that they are like each other, from identical origins. The exact same celestial events but altered evolutions and rates of technological advancement.

"Why were three created, specifically?" Brian wonders.

SOO answers him, "This place was made because there were three spirits who lived and died together, in harmony with God. They knew only the happiness they shared together."

"I've noticed all the universes we have visited have been very different than our boring, huge universe," Calvin says like he wants to say more but doesn't have the words. Then a light goes on, "What is the purpose of our cold and dark universe where life only seems to exist in remote planets?"

SOO clears its nonexistent throat, "Huge universes of physical mystery and vast darkness provide a better chance for more civilizations to evolve their existential awareness, depending on the universe. And, given the chance to prove they can wield power for the benefit of all in their domain, those places can test the common spirit more to inspire great Hope."

"Great question, Calvin. Any others?" Dr. Silver checks with the group.

"What are black holes like here?" Brian wonders.

"Black holes exist but don't cause quite as much havoc. Let's look on our way to a planet," Dr. Silvers tells them.

The IAV shoots into one universe and breaks its barrier like a bubble unbroken. Colors flash pastel in a spectacular dance of heavenly streaks. All stellar movements leave exhaust but dissipate in haste. They find a galaxy with a trail of rainbow dust, and the closer they get, the more each celestial event dazzles the observers than the previous one.

Once they enter the confines of the space egg, the vessel shoots to the center where they approach the vast accretion disk of light around a massive black hole. The colors of fire bleed brightly and the singularity inside makes a noise. A deep bass hum that seems to restart and rev up, like a broken engine.

"Why does this thing behave like it does?" Brian asks. "Seems like it needs to be fixed?"

"SOO, can you explain this phenomenon?" Dr. Silver insists.

SOO answers him, "The black holes in the Triniverse do not function in the traditional manner of swallowing stars. They take their time. These big guys swallow stars, but over great time because they don't have the same gravitational pull as one in your universe. Gravity is different here, as explained before, and so a black hole must work itself up to process its big food."

After a few moments, Dr. Silver tells the group, "Let's go look at a world full of people here." Different species of people travel around in ships and individually from star system to star system.

"This is the most amazing place yet, Dr. Silver," Calvin says. "This is like. I can't put a finger on it. Some go in space alone."

"It really is," Belle agrees with Calvin.

"We're still us, plain as we can see, but these folks are, this place seems imaginary," Calvin adds.

"Dr. Silver, are these people real?" Igbogga asks.

"What is real?" Dr. Silver asks him in return.

"To be real," Calvin replies. "What is Love?" Belle is the only one who gets the joke and the two laugh together.

The IAV flies through dust and clouds to a star system with a large heliosphere. Among the collection of eleven other planets, there is a little blue and green planet with pinks and purples that highlight its aura. The star is a super-giant with a few worlds whose orbits are locked in its safe zone.

"These people live similarly to us on our worlds. All life forms have certain patterns that ensure they can mingle and reproduce, regardless of specifics. All life everywhere and all times knows what Love is and all that goes with it," Dr. Silver tells them as they approach the planet. "It's just that some universes are too chaotic to find it."

"That's sad, and maybe why we all didn't like the worlds in the Dueling Furies one," Calvin says to the doctor.

"If they want to be happy, that is up to them to find it. People blame others too often for their own mistakes and what they don't have in their lives. Like it's up to the rest of us to provide for them."

"No fucking comment," Calvin looks outside to the colors.

They enter its atmosphere, cutting through and viewing the insides of ships and travelers. Inside a small ship, they pass through a large, hairy person who looks unclean. "Not always pretty." Dr. Silver makes a joking gag face.

"Right?" Calvin answers him.

As the IAV descends, traffic of all types crowds the sky but not enough for any disasters. Calvin looks again at a sole traveler and laughs, "That's it! I got it. This place would be cool to come to on

Saturday mornings. Anyone with me?"

"This *is* the Saturday Morning Cartoon Universe, isn't it?" Anna jumps in.

"I love it!" Belle is excited, and sighs with a good exhale. "It's totally television from home."

"What is television?" Igbogga asks Anna.

"Television is a technology that we watch actors or animations, like cartoons, perform stories. We have plays in theaters too, but television is popular," Calvin responds.

"This is fun. I didn't expect a reaction like this. Do any of you have a comparison from your homes to this wonderful place?" Dr. Silver smiles at them.

Allegga speaks up, "We have theater plays that use bright colors like these, but we do not have a technology for watching our actors. Our advancements have centered around space exploration and medicine."

Zyus-Pahl and Whee-Pahl look at each other in awe. Zyus-Pahl looks to the group and speaks up, "We have nothing like what you mention. We have no technology. Well, there were rumors someone had made some kind of weapon that could end the world if they did something, but it was from an unlikely source. The wife and I live a secluded life with our small town and the farm we tended with kin. We only told each other stories. By mouth and by print. This is all so beyond what either of us could have ever imagined in our humble lives.

Dr. Silver responds, "You must really have your eyes wide, then, huh? We'll step outside onto the surface so all of you can feel the texture."

The IAV reaches a secluded area and lands on a patch of smeared looking green grass. The bubble of light emerges from the canopy and encases them, then blends into the colors. The travelers exit the craft and look at their feet and the odd liquidity of the colors.

"Stay inside the bubble," Nurse Goode commands them.

"Yes, everyone MUST stay inside this one. Very important," Dr. Silver looks around.

"Yeah, Whee-Pahl, looking at you!" Calvin smiles at Whee-Pahl and a suspicious Zyus-Pahl.

"Yeah, that was close. I won't do that again, no way," Whee-Pahl assures him.

Dr. Silver walks to the edge of the bubble and turns to the crowd, "Real quickly, I want to point out again that when a universe is made with these physics, less makes sense and therefore some truths are out of reach for life here. We may also have a physical interaction that could rewrite or decompose either us or them. While inside this bubble, we have no effect on the surroundings."

"What type of soul comes here?" Anna asks the shiny doctor.

"The three universes here house, mostly, three different types of souls: the abstract artist, the colorful creative, and the hand wringing writer. This place we are in of the abstract artist where spirits can connect with life forms of all kinds," SOO interjects. "The three universes attract many souls with the gift of expression."

"Are there any giant monsters they contend with anywhere, or is it all pretty colors and happy art?" Zyus-Pahl asks as he and Whee-Pahl walk near the edge of the bubble and lean over to look at the ground to see a nonstop, changing surface. They try to touch it.

"Good question, but no. All life here is around 20 times our size or smaller, which is standard. Fewer universes have those mammoth giants like in Aquaverse," Dr. Silver says and then looks at the Zor-ahns and points to them, "Please, please. You two, let's walk it back a bit." The two gentle folks back up two steps and turn to the doctor, who looks back to the rest of the group.

"It would be more fun to interact with them," Calvin hints to the doctor.

"No, can't. These people wouldn't understand any of you. Your voices might boom with truth that could break any of them into nothing." As Dr. Silver says those words, Zyus-Pahl missteps on Whee-Pahl's foot and loses his balance.

CRACK! His back goes out and he falls outside the bubble while he catches his balance! "Aagh!" Zyus-Pahl's feet interact with the outside surface in a strange way, then...

"Zyus!" Whee-Pahl jumps out and grabs Zyus-Pahl. They both contact the ground and cause it to draw out lines and graph the land into thin, green lines. The two freeze in their places with pleas on their faces. Locals all around them scream and fly away.

"LOOK! It's The Lost! Let's go!" Dr. Silver yells as the giant ghost throws a ball— BOOM! The ball hits the ground near the IAV and then returns to her.

Calvin follows the rest of them to the craft but looks for a second if he do anything. Belle grabs his arm and they go inside to their seats.

"Get in the IAV immediately. Everyone! Zyus, Whee!" Nurse Goode says as the group runs to the ship. "We must save them, Doctor."

"We have to leave them!" Dr. Silver exclaims.

The Lost zooms closer and fills the sky. She winds up her hand, and misses as the doors shut behind Nurse Goode and the energy bubble retracts. The Lost's hand contacts Zyus-Pahl and Whee-Pahl as the IAV flees.

The craft flies out of the world's view, and out of the star system, but then a force slows them down. They are still, then they shoot straight to the edge of the universe and find themselves in a large catalog of universes.

They fly backwards and then stop. The pattern of white squares grows and encloses them in a room. The same room as before. The group sits in a circle, with two empty seats. SOO looks around at the group but does not speak.

"Uh, Doctor, is this the same." Calvin is cut off.

The white squares above them shrink, and a craft, with strange beings, stares at the group. Some of the patients are frozen in shock, while others are fidgety and off center. Then two figures descend from the mysterious craft above: Zyus-Pahl and Whee-Pahl!

"Hey! Zyus-Pahl and Whee-Pahl!" Belle is excited to see their friends.

The group is audible in their pleasantries, and the mysterious wonder above retreats before the travelers can look back up. That is, except for Dr. Silver and Nurse Goode, of course. The room becomes whole again and lights up.

Dr. Silver motions to the Zor-ahns, "Welcome back, you two. We will resume this trip now that we learned that lesson." He winks at the group, "Remember, we need to obey all rules, and I know that won't be an issue going forward."

"This feels like a joke I made already." Calvin smirks.

"You are so funny, skinny man," Zyus-Pahl nudges him in comradery. Brian sees Calvin smile at the ram-like man and shows his distance to them.

"We all set?" Dr. Silver looks at everyone, then hits his tablet. The room darkens, and the canopy surrounds around them again, then it transforms back into the IAV. Belle goes below without a peep. Calvin does so as well and then the rest join them. "I guess we'll take a break and come back refreshed."

Dr. Silver and Nurse Goode remain.

"I like this group. Kind of spicy," Nurse Goode says.

"Yeah, I like Calvin. Something about him."

The IAV flies into the massive catalog of universes, then enters a structure with soothing lights and sounds. He parks the craft and the silver beings go below.

PART TWO

Chapter 8: Some Quick Stops Along the 10th Dimension

Suspended within the hidden structure and adorned with soft lighting and peaceful music, the IAV has an empty canopy. The ten travelers emerge in their own timing, a mellow return to a heavy experience. Once all ten are there, the vessel unlocks from the dock and coasts out to the great selection area of visual complexity that is sufficient evidence of divine creation.

All around them, the encapsulating carousel of various universes circles them at a digestible speed. Then, one by one, the rows stop. Everything is different, from colors and shapes to perspective and polarity, define each one. Scrambling through the limitless assortment, the Instantly Adaptable Vehicle locks on one specific universe and shoots into it.

The scales of size and movement daze the people as they change to the correct proportion and pass whole galaxies like they're a piece of dust. The universe appears vast and dark with hints of light and mass to be found.

Dr. Silver turns to the group and says, "From here, in the 10th Dimension," then he shoots Brian a wink. The doctor continues, "We are now going to tour four random universes that are quite odd and not really what a realm should be. The first one, which we just entered, is vast and dark with very isolated stars and galaxies."

"This sounds like ours," Brian says as he looks around.

"It's not. Ooh, look at that star over there." The doctor points to a star nearby and they all focus on it. The light of the huge star changes from white yellow to full orange, then a red hand reaches out.

"What?" Calvin can't believe it. "What is that?"

"They have many names on many worlds, but they are mainly referred to as Star Borns."

Calvin has light bulb moment and raises his finger, "Uh, wait, I just thought of something. What were those creatures who dropped off Zyus-Pahl and Whee-Pahl?"

Dr. Silver is surprised, "Calvin, good catch. They were part of the Collection."

"Interesting." Calvin thinks he is on to something.

Nurse Goode speaks up, "If we can all turn our attention outside?"

The Star Born reaches out of its womb and draws the entirety of the star into its body. Its face is gloriously beautiful, with yellow and red coloring. The giant gathers itself to gain balance in the middle of empty space. Then, it takes off running! It moves through the galaxy as it scans the cosmos.

"Now, that's a Starman. What does something like that eat?" Belle asks.

"We may see soon since it's a new one. It needs matter in large scales. We're about to watch it here at this asteroid belt of another star system."

"This is pretty cool, right?" Calvin looks at Belle, who nods in awe.

The Star Born finds a gas giant with rings of rock and debris. It moves close and swallows some grub. Then, it sticks its head inside the gas giant and inhales the gas until there is only a small mass in the middle. The Star Born smells the mass and whiffs, then goes on its way.

"Rock planets and moons. When he stuck his head in the gas giant — we call that a gas oven. They're fun to watch, don't you think? SOO, any details?"

SOO lights up, "Yes, Dr. Silver. This large being feeds off everything that makes planets and moons but are careful to avoid taking life. They are only born from rogue stars because any star in a system will stay unborn if life is possible. They are like guardians of this universe."

"Thank you, SOO. That was interesting, wasn't it? Any questions?" The doctor looks around.

"Another one is coming from over there," Anna says.

"That is a full grown one," Dr. Silver says to her.

The second giant, with less yellow and redder, is larger and dimmer. It meets the newborn and they greet each other in a full hug. They communicate in their own language, then go towards another gas giant. The IAV follows them.

When the two reach the ringed gas planet, they look all around it and then the rest of the system. "Must not be any life in this system," Dr. Silver guesses. The giants grab some small moons and gobble them, then one laughs and swipes away the rings. As the rings disappear, they laugh again.

"These two are having a good old time, huh?" Calvin laughs.

The elder giant reaches into the gas planet and pulls out the core with dripping metal. They wipe the metal away and into their mouths, then one bites half off and gives it to the other.

"Wild, wild stuff," Calvin looks at Belle.

"Like a dripping strawberry," Belle says to him.

"Looks like a baby Ellagantce," Dr. Silver says as the two lose their place in the flirt. "Any questions about this place before we move on to the next one?"

"What are the normal people like here?" Allegga asks.

"SOO, what are the hominids like here?" Dr. Silver asks the sentient orb.

"The life here are aware of the great Star Borns but do not wish to travel in space because they do not fully understand them. It is a phenomenon across the entire universe." Dr. Silver looks at his tablet and continues, "Any questions before we move on?"

"Oh, so, the people aren't worth seeing?" Calvin pushes the doctor.

"Not that. There's nothing new. How about we go to the next one?" Dr. Silver works the controls.

The IAV shoots out of the one odd realm and enters a new, mysterious one. Stars and planets, bare and still, fly along orbits and seem like an average, regular universe. It *looks* like it has all the elements of a universe, but the deficit is clearer upon a closer look.

Nurse Goode points to her tablet and says, "I think we should do this one last."

The doctor huddles with the nurse, "We'll just do this one here since we're already here. I'm not concerned with the order of these four." Dr. Silver turns to the group, "This place is different from all the others. You'll see, there are no forms of life here, just matter and celestial objects of most kinds here. Spirits do live here, though."

"How do spirits live here?" Belle asks the host.

"I want to show you."

The vessel moves through the realm, passing galaxies and stars of enormous size, then it zooms in closer to a star system. They fly to the surface of a planet, through a thin atmosphere of dust and clouds, to a clear planet, below. The craft lands in an open spot with piles of dirt and rubble scattered around.

"I don't see anything, Doc," Calvin says as they look around.

"Just watch," The doctor says as a swath of land gathers up and smacks a small hill. The small hill caves in a bit, then turns up and the two gatherings of rock smack each other in a violent duel. "Thoughts?"

"Waves of rocks fighting each other? This is weird," Brian is confused.

"What's the point of this?" Igbogga asks.

"The point is I wanted to show you all what life does for the many spirits, and how important it is to have a balance between material energy and spiritual energy. Oh, and the correct set of elements in a universe that can foster life. I believe there's no Nitrogen, Phosphorus, and Sulfur here. Right, SOO?"

SOO answers him, "That's right, Nitrogen, Phosphorus, and Sulfur are three of five elements necessary to create life and they do not exist here. This place was created to punish sadistic torturers of many universes. You see how violent their nature is towards each other? That is a derelict spirit."

"This place may be a similar sentence as the universe of the Dueling something," Zyus-Pahl says.

"The Dueling Furies, yes, in a sense that it is an awful fate to inherit, but the main reason it is bad here is that no spirit here can die to leave. They are all trapped in their inorganic rock piles and hills. Some may become stars and planets themselves, but they can never leave."

"Why is sadistic torturing so heavily punished?" Calvin asks.

"SOO?" The doctor turns it over to the sphere.

"Because when you torture another life form, the pain and suffering within that life form passes onto God," SOO says in an even tone. "Within the event of torture, the victim reaches a level of helplessness when they begin to feel as though they should give up. God is connected to all life, so it can inspire strength in others who may be decent enough to stand up for the compromised. The imbalance worsens when some commit atrocities, because they can."

There is silence in the canopy. Nurse Goode taps the doctor on the shoulder and whispers to him. Belle goes down below.

"Yes, let's move on. Thank you, Nurse Goode. Any thoughts?"

Brian asks him, "Is there is a different universe for each type of bad deed? Like, is there a universe of no fire for the spirits who were pyros?"

Dr. Silver answers him, "Maybe, Brian. We won't be going to anymore universes now that have been created for the punishment of derelict souls. We still have a few, but they are all on the wonder side of awe. We are now going to go the third universe of this segment."

The IAV leaves the universe in haste and returns to the catalog of realms. The choices amaze Allegga and Igbogga as they stare around. Allegga says, "So much life must be out there."

"I know, imagine all of the lovely beings there are to meet," Igbogga replies to his mate.

Brian's disapproving look catches Anna's attention. "What's wrong, Brian?"

"Nothing."

"It must suck to have to judge others so much before you allow yourself to look within and let go."

"Whatever," Brian mutters.

"Well said, Anna," Dr. Silver nods to her.

Belle returns to the group and is welcomed with a smile from Calvin. "What did I miss?" She asks Dr. Silver.

"Just a little discussion," The doctor assures her.

The IAV zeros in on another universe and darts, but the moment they enter, they are blasted with light. So much white light with yellow flashes startle everyone, even the hosts. The craft stops in its tracks.

"What is going on here?" Calvin asks the doctor.

"Sorry, let me adjust the canopy," Dr. Silver hits a few buttons on the console, and the canopy changes to a dark tint. Millions and billions of stars fill the deepest space to illuminate galaxies and worlds. "How's that? SOO, some facts about this universe as to why it is so bright?"

SOO replies, "Yes, this universe has over 8,000 times the number of stars in a hundredth of the space, compared to the one our eight patients originate. Black holes have plenty to feast on, but the number of stars here cause many collisions and even more light. Life happens anyway, though, as rock planets wait for an icy comet or meteor to collide and microbes comes about and evolve." SOO looks around, "You know blah, blah, blah, yadda."

Calvin is confused and asks, "How does ice stay ice with so many stars?"

SOO answers, "There are many stars that have a heliosphere large enough to contain ample ice and rocks for comets. Water will travel from time to time. Different physics than your home, Calvin Wayne."

"Any chance space travelers and advanced societies here bargain for or even steal ice or water?" Calvin asks. "Like pirates?"

"Possibly, Calvin, but let's not worry about icy empires and pirates right now," Dr. Silver winks at Calvin. "One thing here I want to mention that may differ from many other realms is that life always looks for the darkness to come alive. Any developed life here, SOO?"

"Some life here has advanced to space travel, taking caverns in planets to make bases and expand their reach, yet they can only do so much. The violent nature of so many stars in so many trajectories prohibits extensive space travel."

"Thank you, SOO. We're just about done here, are there any observations or questions?"

Anna speaks up first, "I pray I never have to live here."

"I will just say, this place gives you no privacy!" Belle jokes.

"Yeah, I'm good with this place," Calvin agrees.

"Good thing is that life here does not suffer. There are many places and varieties of things in those places that the extreme light is only a mere nuisance. Let's move on to the fourth quick visit, the Rainbow Universe."

The IAV shoots out of the brightness and into the catalog reality, where everyone blinks and rubs their eyes. A selection is made before the travelers can register the sequence. They enter a new realm in a colored spark and appear in a fantastic place of colors and white light.

"This is a bit different, Doc. A lot of color," Calvin says and then stares out at the new realm.

"Yes, and I wanted you all to see what happens when a universe has too much carbon and plenty of pressure. Sometimes, universes are just beautiful," Dr. Silver shrugs and hits some buttons on the console, and the IAV takes off into the colors.

They pass rainbow shooting galaxies and down into a gas cloud of green and violet. Through the gases, they find a star in its safety cloud to visit. As they enter the star's neighborhood, diamond planets reflect their own lines along the spectrum of colors.

One planet is different, whose rock and flora give it away as a life giver. As they approach the world, the hues blend into the light blue atmosphere.

"I think it's disco time," Calvin says to Belle and Anna. The three begin to goof off in a disco dance, so Dr. Silver hits a button to start some disco music. A mirror ball appears above and lights spin around them.

"I want to join in," Allegga starts to move.

"Oh, me too, me too," Igbogga joins them.

Brian and the Zor-ahns remain still and without fun, but for different reasons. Zyus-Pahl speaks up, "I guess Zor-ahns are the only ones here who don't dance? We do it in private as part of our together ritual."

They groove for a minute on the way.

"There are plenty of planets to visit, but I saved this one to show you because of its inherent beauty and people with basic, but not advanced, technology they have had for many generations. These folks live at peace," Dr. Silver explains as they fly into the planet's atmosphere.

The IAV descends to the surface and coasts through a landscape of greenery, with many shades of colors in the flowers and bushes. People make their way out of hiding. Then, the craft slows down above a village of people, all of whom have food and smiles.

"They look like they're partying, right?" Belle asks.

"I think they just look happy," Anna says. "It looks so refreshing and cleansing to see such enjoyment without a world of hectic hustling."

Some of the people who are not joining in the fun are doing chores and taking care of things all about, but none with a frown. Maybe it smells good everywhere too.

"These lucky guys and gals here live in the moment because they have no worry of the future and their past is without much pain. Much to be said for this way of existing," Dr. Silver explains. "Any questions, issues, or concerns?"

"I think I'm good with these, not much to discuss," Brian tries to impede the therapy.

"Let's see if anyone else has a word," Nurse Goode looks around.

"I liked that the last people here live in the moment. I know, in my happiest times, I am living in the moment and experiencing each second with my senses," Calvin expresses this and looks at Belle.

"That is so true, Calvin. I liked the beauty of the planet here, it was so Eden-like," Belle says with joy.

Nurse Goode nods at Dr. Silver. He speaks up, "I showed you these four specific universes to teach you how different life can be," Dr. Silver says.

The IAV leaves the planet's surface and flies up into the stars and rainbows. Once they reach the balance between darkness and light, they can see many hues everywhere.

"Any more thoughts on these places as they pertain to your suffering?"

Belle goes next, "This one was good, but the others were unpleasant. I hope I never have to survive in them." She drops below.

"I thought they were wild and yeah, never want to live in any of these places unless I'm one of the big giants born from stars," Brian says.

Allegga jumps in, "So far, I would only want to live in a peaceful universe. Ig?"

Igbogga responds, "Oh yes, me as well. It's scary out here, except the last one."

"Well, I'm glad you said that because we are going to start a new series right now of three different universes, and they were made in the most interesting way." Dr. Silver continues, "So, I please go below and take a few moments to relax. If you want to entertain yourself, program your tablet."

The IAV darts to the edge of the universe and leaves in small spot...

Chapter 9: Creators- Haze Universe

Swirling colors in dust and light, with hues of yellows and purples and some orange and blue, dazzle the expanse. Hypnotic vibrations and rhythms fill this cosmos with an unavoidable jam session conducted by a great spirit in the shadows of a super cluster. Comets on their paths and orbits cast out surgical guitar riffs as the spirit's deep voice harmonizes into blooming emotions of bliss.

Galaxies spin and glow to the beat, then on their own, and all back together as energies help illuminate all corners of this peaceful place. But then a large moon shoots out of one galaxy to loop around another's rings and return. Another moon does it.

In a poof of colorful stardust, the IAV enters the spectacular realm. As they move inward, Dr. Silver speaks to the group, "Ah, yes. Welcome everyone to the Haze Universe, as it has been dubbed. We'll check out a black hole and some phenomenon first."

Another moon shoots around a ring and returns to it host galaxy. Belle smiles and sings in a talking voice, "1, 2, 3, 4, 5, 6, 7, 8, 9, 10— "

"11, 12," Calvin finishes and they high five with a laugh.

"Did I miss something?" Allegga asks them.

"These two, I think, are referring to a show when they were kids, right?"

"I think it's a cartoon or a puppet show," Calvin seems foggy.

"Yeah, Muppet Show or Sesame Street, or Electric Company, or something," Anna adds.

"I don't want to say the incorrect one, I've had arguments over this very thing," Belle says as she sits back in her seat.

There is a short pause, then Dr. Silver chimes in, "Excellent! There's always something new." He and Nurse Goode smile along with them. Back to the controls, Dr. Silver accelerates the vessel.

They fly through the colors and speed to the closest galaxy with a black hole at its center. As they approach it, they can see the yellow accretion disk and instead of black at the event horizon, it is purple shooting out and with black, peaking from behind it, inside.

"Black holes are cool to study in each universe but wonder how this 'Group Therapy for so-and-so Methods or Reasons' is all supposed to make me feel better inside after I lost all of the love in my life."

Dr. Silver replies, "Sometimes, Brian, you need to speak about the issues, like you just did, and you will figure it out. Everyone here is different, and for Belle with a physical disease, we'll discuss other avenues in a bit. No one can replace a loved one, Brian, but beautiful souls of all orientations exist here and back on Earth. It is up to you to find them and make the best of each moment."

"Yeah, well."

"That's kind of part of what I need to learn, Doc. I mean, my racing thoughts and occasional hallucinations distract me from the moment quite often, and I find myself playing catchup with conversations and many things in life when I'm alone. It can be painful because I have lost many genuine connections because of it. It's not as if I was intentionally zoning out. Maybe it can be about being grateful for each of those moments, and letting some things go, rather than dissecting each one to boredom."

"Wow, Calvin," Belle grabs Calvin's hand.

"Yes, Calvin, thank you for sharing that. You have so much to offer others. Some of those thoughts lie behind the mental blocks of the next generation of people and elderly folks who refused internal growth," Dr. Silver looks at the dancing colors outside and back at Calvin with a smile. He continues, "I think it is about facing your pain without fear of its hold on you and your dreams."

There is silence as they all look outside to the drug-free acid trip.

"Why is it called the Haze Universe?" Anna asks.

"Anna, the Haze Universe is named after the Creator of this universe, a man from 20th century Earth named Jimi Hendrix. It explains why there are so many abstract elements to this place, from the colors to the rhythms."

"Jimi Hendrix?" Calvin can't believe it. "What do you mean? Jimi Hendrix is the God of this universe? And that spirit over there in his groove is HIM?"

"There is only One God, but many universes have Creators, who exist within the framework of all existence. And, yes, that's him there making his magic. For many universes, to better manage life, there is a former life form that has been elevated. It is called 'Super Individualization', and after you become a Creator, you can never live a normal life in another universe again. You can do so alone or with one or two others."

"Jimi Hendrix has only been dead since the 70's and his universe is already developed? How does that work?" Brian doesn't believe it at all.

Dr. Silver smiles and points to SOO, "Can you take this one?"

SOO answers, "Each universe can develop at whatever speed the Creator wishes. Jimi Hendrix made this place in a matter of hours. His genius in life was a substantial connection to The One, so his choices met few obstacles. Free spirits come here to live in harmony with a great Creator, to have abundance without any greed and hoarding by those in power."

"Are any of us going to get the option of becoming a Creator?" Calvin asks.

"Perhaps, Calvin. You may get the option to learn some knowledge beyond any treasure as you become a Creator. However, there are other universes where life is not mortal, and we'll get to a couple of those too. But, as a Creator, you can design all laws of physics, build worlds, and provide for life to evolve and grow. We need to make sure you are not sadistic but instead have specific good qualities."

"So, what are the people like in Jimi's place?" Belle asks.

"Yes, let's travel in a bit closer." Dr. Silver turns around and hits the controls. The IAV shoots into one of the galaxies and to a star system. As they pass through a wall of heat and fire unaffected, there are a few worlds that glow blue or green or purple. The craft aims at a world and cruises to it. He continues, "Let's look at this world right here. It has a decent standard of living and some other features."

The craft glides to the planet and through its atmosphere, which reveals a plentiful world of flora and fauna. There is no evidence of an overbearing civilization pushing aside the bountiful landscape, except some huts of different sizes.

"SOO, can you give us some relevant facts about this pretty garden?" Dr. Silver lands in the middle of a large area of green grass and flowers.

People walk about, dressed in natural clothing to a meeting place of tables and a stage. Hunters carry a carcass to a large hut, and a crowd brings fruits and veggies to the tables. Everyone is light and easy.

SOO lights up, "Yes, Dr. Silver. The dominant species here live in harmony with all others because they need only enough to survive. No war exists here or any other planet in this efficient universe, which is a result of two things: a) all species who govern, do so with the wisdom of experience, abundance, and compromise, and b) no species possesses enough specialized intelligence to advance any legitimate technology." SOO looks around and smiles.

"I want to add that Jimi Hendrix was alive and performing his music in a time of controversial war with another country. Musicians got together to protest but the war machine was unstoppable," Calvin goes on. "It makes sense that Mr. Hendrix would be honored with this awesome destiny and would make a place so groovy."

"Thank you, Calvin. And SOO. Okay, this universe has no other real differences to teach, so I want to ask about everyone's problems and health issues. Big talk or small talk. Let's start with Brian. How are you at this point?"

"I miss the Earth, I miss my wife," he pauses and rubs his head. "She was just my everything. Ah, forget it. I lost so much, but I still don't want to lose it in front of all of you. I think I'm fine now, though."

"I'm sorry for your pain, Brian. Loss is always difficult, especially when it's someone close to you." Dr. Silver reads his tablet.

Brian brushes it off with an expression of feelings stuffed down inside. He toughens up and puts on a face, "Whatever. I'll get over it, like I got through everything else in my life. At least I have great health, for the most part." He looks at Calvin, "At least I'm not sick in the head."

Calvin catches himself from reacting and turns his head. When he looks back, Dr. Silver is staring at him. Calvin says to the doctor, "I wish we could get out of the IAV in a remote area of greenery so you could all watch me beat the snot out of this punk."

Brian smiles and is about to reply, but Dr. Silver jumps in, "Okay, you two healing people. Please refrain from animosity and the antagonism of others. Clear?"

Calvin looks at Brian without emotion and back at the doctor, "Of course."

"Sure," Brian goes to his console and makes a foaming beer. Others stare at him and drink from their glasses without a word.

"There are better people here, eight of them, I'd rather focus on," Calvin nods at the doctor.

The IAV remains as locals walk around and celebrate being alive. A paradise of sorts where animals of all kinds live alongside the people. The foliage delights the senses with smells and colors that hypnotize. The water runs blue and clear, depending on depth.

"Belle, how is your midsection holding up on the trip?" Dr. Silver asks her.

"It's been fine for the most part, but I don't think I really ever expect perfection." Belle puts on a firm face.

"Can we help or offer anything to improve comfort?"

"I eat when I'm hungry and I've been on this diet for some time. I have my pills here; it's a tough situation. Painful and frustrating and disgusting."

"Yes, it is a terrible disease that exists on other worlds. Like lupus and a few others. Something with certain species that develop and the body fights itself. Rest assured, it is a common health problem — disease. Next, how about you, Igbogga?"

"I'm fine, sleeping normally. This adventure has done wonders for me. I now feel more aware of the greater part of existence you are introducing us to everywhere we've gone."

"I'm glad to hear, Igbogga. Great news. Allegga, how about you?"

"This has all been so enjoyable and great. We never dreamed of this type of journey. No one thinks they'll be given an opportunity like this," Allegga is happy as they describe the experience.

"Glad to hear about you too, Allegga. Anna, how have you been doing?" Dr. Silver asks her.

"I don't know. Kind of okay, this has all been very, um, it's expanded my attention enough for me to minimize that pain that was just so overwhelming and blinding before. I'm still trying to process all of my pain and regain the happiness I had before. I remember how beautiful some days were, regardless of the weather, and I felt like God was shining on me and I was in the right place at the right time."

"Wow, I really hope I can help you get back to where you were. I think it's where you belong. And Calvin- how are you feeling right now?"

"All of these places and lessons have inspired me to give a stronger voice to the shy but decent side of me. I always faced my head problems head on but never felt more capable of overcoming my issues than at this point. My moods simmer inside, so even when I don't show it, I could be swaying back and forth. Wait, do you have any advanced medicine for any of us that could use it?" Calvin wonders. "It seems like we could make any medicine here in the IAV that could help cure us, couldn't we?

"Thank you, Calvin, glad to hear you find strength. And good question- you may be able to program it to your exact DNA, but the change may make you feel foreign within yourself because you are used to the chaos inside. You may feel bored, or you may become obsessive, or you may do fine. Probably there is no chance of that for those with physical diseases. It's up to you, Calvin. Many of your other issues will need therapy or are minor enough that we will address them all by the completion of our time together."

"Yeah, maybe I will just wait until later." Calvin looks at the others to see some minds open to the chance.

"Zyus-Pahl, would you like to try a cure for your dry skin? Igbogga, your cysts, and Brian, you can take something. Belle, you can take something for your Crohn's disease and acid reflux. Varicose veins, and so on. Unfortunately, many of your problems require therapy plus medication to undo and rewire your thinking," Dr. Silver says to them as medicine bottles appear on their consoles.

Zyus-Pahl gets excited, "I'm going to try it right now." He grabs his tube of medicine with an elder's curiosity, an examination the others find somewhat amusing. He squeezes a white ointment onto his fingers and smothers his hands and feet, then shakes his smiling head and drops below.

Igbogga, Brian, Anna, and Belle all grab their new medicine and take a dosage, without any hesitation. Igbogga doesn't like to take pills but pushes themselves anyway.

Belle massages her stomach and closes her eyes in a moment of relaxation. She breathes a couple of times and brings her attention back to the group.

"Why didn't you offer them these cures right off the bat once we started traveling? Belle has been suffering," Calvin says as the others wait for an answer.

"I was planning on providing them in the next universe where it is a touch more peaceful, but it is all good. Oh, and, if you become a Creator, all common issues that hamper the living are gone. All that goes with the Creator is their Self, Will, Artistic Ability, and Personality." Dr. Silver nods and looks around.

"Why not Intelligence?" Brian asks him.

"Creators are endowed with intelligence beyond any life form. For example, remember one ability, from a bit ago, that they develop is to create entire systems of physical laws and sciences in a way that the universe can remain stable, as we have seen so far." Dr. Silver checks his tablet, and they lift off the planet, back into heavy metal deep space. "Any objections that we go to the next stop in our journey? We'll further discuss the five with their cures in the next plane."

"I think we're ready, Captain Stubin," Calvin smirks, and the other Humans giggle.

Belle points at Calvin with two fingers and smiles, "Outta sight!" Anna and Calvin both crack up, supported by a dominating levity. Brian holds back his smile.

"Stubin?" Dr. Silver is confused and shrugs his shoulders. He turns around, and the vessel shoots straight to the edge of space... POOF!

Chapter 10: Creators- Sweet Dreams Universe

It is a beautiful day of blue skies all around, including many plump clouds on random journeys. Birds of many sizes and colors and types are free between worlds, mostly comprised of water and rock. People of many origins fly without any thought of danger or doom, blessed by their sweet Lord who lets them dream away. Small showers and storms drift by planets and stars to project rainbows across the realm.

Lush planets and bright, benign stars in fields of galaxies have grown throughout this universe with the same atmosphere: one with air to spare everywhere. Spaceships look more like planes and blimps than rockets or disks.

Along the outer edges of the universe, deep blue hues hide the boundaries from the abundant life. The IAV emerges from a tiny opening in the air, with a small trail of purple dust, prepared to discover this new realm. "I would like to welcome you all to the Sweet Dreams Universe. It's by another Creator, another artist born on Earth in the 20th century, George Harrison," Dr. Silver says.

"George Harrison? Are you kidding me?" Belle is excited.

"I can see it," Calvin says in agreement. "Do all popular musicians become Creators, Dr. Silver? Or should I say, 'Rock Gods'?"

"It depends. Some are dark and disturbed and would not fit as one," Dr. Silver answers him.

Zyus-Pahl's light bulb goes on, and he asks, "Wait, Doctor. These artists are dead and ascended, as you say it. Does that mean we are dead? Is this the life beyond life, as we have in our stories?"

Whee-Pahl becomes excited and asks another question before

anyone else, "Is there any chance we are still alive? We are eating and taking medicine."

"I am happy to say that we are all alive and relatively well. Well enough for this trip. But, when life forms die, they are reborn or elevated. Since we are alive and, on this journey, we are fortunate enough to choose where we end up. And, with a full arsenal of experiences relevant to your preferred destiny," Dr. Silver smiles at them.

Brian gives a hint of skepticism, then says, "Did you drug us?"

Nurse Goode puts her hand on Dr. Silver's, and answers, "We don't drug anyone. Everyone has access to medication that they need. I'm starting to think we should change the policy."

"Okay, Nurse. Let's continue," the doctor replies.

"Yes, of course. I will return in a few minutes," Nurse Goode goes down into her chamber, then Belle follows, then the rest follow.

"I guess another break. Oh well. SOO, keep an eye out and let me know if we have an issue," Dr. Silver says to the orb.

SOO smiles back and replies, "Like a nosy neighbor."

The group returns from the rest, but they are quiet. Belle and Calvin make eye contact, and share a subtle but gentle grin.

"There are no dark and stormy days here in this place, and no ice or snow. Well, there IS snow on certain worlds where it gets just cold enough for it to stick but warm enough to enjoy it," Dr. Silver looks at his tablet. "Let's move about."

The IAV cruises through the blue space and some of the clouds, as the passengers watch people fly around in delight. Stars burn warm and have orbiting nondestructive structures tended to by locals.

"Dr. Silver— I just got notice," Nurse Goode hits a button and Dr. Silver reads his tablet.

The doctor responds, "Oh, great news! I have a surprise for all of you. Let's just go there and we'll let it speak for itself."

They zoom into a galaxy nearby and through some clouds to a star system with ten green planets. As the craft approaches one of the worlds, they see structures in its orbit that house large propeller machines. The surface begins to reveal large bodies of water, mountains and flat plains, waterfalls and steady rains. As they cruise to a stop in a meadow, it is evident they are in a place like home.

Calvin can't contain himself, "This place is awesome!"

"Totally," Belle says. Allegga and Igbogga agree.

"And, we haven't even gotten to the surprise yet. Here, we can leave the IAV, but it will be camouflaged as one of theirs to the locals. And only we can enter it. One quick thing— I want you all to be grownups and no go too far from the group, but you can all fly here," Dr. Silver tells them. "If you don't behave though, you may spoil it for the rest of us." They all chuckle.

"Actually, both Igbogga and I can fly in most atmospheres," Allegga adds.

"That's cool. I can't wait to see what it's like," Calvin says.

The IAV transforms into a common home as it lands behind a secluded hill, also becoming visible. The door opens on the side, and the passengers exit in a hurry. The local people are of many different species and styles of clothing, so no one pays them much attention.

"Alright, have fun flying," Dr. Silver tells them.

The four Humans go into the open area together and watch around at others lifting off the ground, but they do so without the fuss. Allegga and Igbogga jump up and fly around together. Calvin smiles at them, nods some belief into himself, then runs up into the air without a problem.

Calvin is free, "Oh my God, this so cool! It's easier than it looks." His glee shines as he spins and twirls, then he floats above the group. "That was so fun. Belle, you have to try it."

"Okay, here goes nothing," Belle says as she runs and jumps into the air without much of a struggle. Anna runs in her own direction, jumps, and shots way up in the air. Brian sees her and takes his jump with ease, then flies around. The four Humans are out of their wits, overcome with the common dream ability.

Calvin and Belle then go off together while the group remains near the craft. Belle shoots ahead and then upward into what she would think is space. Calvin follows her in a great arc through clear air. They stop above the beautiful planet and its wild, beautiful colors.

"Let's look around, Belle."

"Sure."

They hold hands from up high, looking at another world, they've seen, and this one is a special one. The couple then drifts down together into a hovering float, above an area of plush, grassy plains to fields of wildflowers. "I'm really having a good time," Calvin smiles with her.

"This planet is so perfect," Belle exhales and sighs.

"Wait, is it perfect enough to get a kiss?" Calvin holds his hand out to her.

"It is."

In mid-flight, Calvin and Belle hold hands, and he leans in to meet her for a tender kiss, with no one around disturbing them. They hold each other with sweet consideration, and Calvin whispers, "Is your stomach okay?"

"Yes, thank you, Calvin."

"Let's land for a minute." They land near the edge of the forest and sit on a makeshift table. Flowers and reeds of grain fill the land.

"I don't like to mess around with just anyone, Belle. My mental illness makes things difficult, and I want you to know that my extreme emotions are about me and just a wall. If I have an issue, it's behind that wall, and I have to try to communicate with you over that wall."

"I totally get it. It can't be easy to have such a serious disorder. For me, it's just about if a guy can tolerate being with a woman who has gas like mine and the smell from the bathroom is nearly unbearable at times."

"Everyone poops," Calvin smiles at her.

"Yeah, I know. It's nice to talk with someone who can talk about health problems. Life is hard enough to have to pretend to everyone else that I'm tough and can take it."

"Now you're speaking my language. I've lost many friends who thought I was selfish or a whiner or whatever because I was in this horrible place psychologically and needed a friend. It's tough."

Calvin reaches out and grabs Belle's hand. She reaches back and they smile as they close in for another delicate kiss.

"Being with you isn't tough," Belle says softly.

"It's like a dream right now. The circumstances and you, it's just awesome," Calvin looks deep in her eyes and they embrace. "Do you want to go back yet? They may be looking for us."

"Yeah, I guess. Do you want to maybe 'go below' together in the IAV? Good thing we're already next to each other." Belle wonders.

"Let's go back right now."

They jump in the air, then zoom back over the scenery to the inter-dimensional craft, where their fellow aliens wait for them. The duo lands and follows the others inside.

"Dr. Silver said he was going to leave you two," Anna jokes.

"I was not going to leave them. Oh, I get it." Dr. Silver now gets it. He closes the doors behind the new couple, who take their seats. "We're going to lift off this world, so if anyone objects, let me know."

Calvin smiles, "That was fun. Flying, in that way, is something I could do all the time. It's like your center of gravity moves by your mind's will. Really something."

"I'm glad we didn't have any problems with any super beings," Zyus-Pahl adds.

"Yes, Zyus-Pahl. I agree. The Lost will not bother us again, as we will only travel to more advanced places than those earlier ones. We will go to one more Creator's Universe, then a few we will go where a certain wrong action could bring Aurfuud."

They lift off into the light blue space and pass a happy little cloud here and there. People fly through the expanse to planets of all types, and to stations they have built where there are no nearby stars or worlds.

Dr. Silver turns around and looks up from his tablet, "Okay, any questions about this universe?"

"It makes sense that this is George Harrison's universe. It's totally beautiful and harmonious. I could live here," Calvin says.

"Dr. Silver, do Creators that live as an individual life form become mortal in some way? Or as a super powerful being?" Brian asks him.

"Yes, like a Primary soul, they can live as a mortal life form, but they must stay anonymous. However, they retain the awareness and intelligence endowed with them and must never be murdered or crucified. It doesn't kill that Creator, but when a species uses that symbol to control their own population, they wander from the light and create an imbalance on their world. Humility, honesty, and benevolence must be honored for a species to reach a true collective enlightenment."

"Earth is certainly imbalanced," Anna says with a tired exhale. "People like to spread lies like 'there is no good and evil, there's just money and power', it really gets under my skin."

Brian looks angry, "I don't know if I agree with everything you said there, Doctor. God wants me to be as great as I can be and look after my own. That is all. I don't owe anyone anything. I can see if you start a universe, this is insane, and you want there to be harmony. I want harmony and balance and all that good stuff too, but there's always someone out there to ruin the party. Someone must climb that mountain and plant their flag because someone else is already on their way to do it as well and I don't want to be in their shadow."

"Interesting viewpoint, Brian. Any thoughts, anyone?" Dr. Silver looks around.

Allegga looks at their partner and says, "Brian, I live for Igbogga, and I feel it. Feel it, deep inside that they love and live for me the same way. Perhaps you felt that for your late wife. But realize that you don't have to believe in what I experience for it to be real, and the opposite is true as well. We live a bountiful and luxurious lifestyle with power to share and resources to spare. Selfishness is what you describe, as it sounds to me, and you are allowed to live such an existence, but why not share?"

"Most people I have ever known, on Earth that is, have betrayed me or I lost them. It's like I only know disappointment and loss. Sadness with no one who can comfort me. Me and Danielle, we were so good together. We both helped each other plan in a practical way, but not to obsess over it. And, then she was gone. I didn't plan for the being alone part. You are strangers, well, I don't know what you've been through, but I don't believe in much of what others say."

There is a short silence, and a few eyes look outside the IAV at the travelers and the clear sky.

Dr. Silver lights up, "Well, Brian, we all learn and open in our own time. You never know when you will experience a breakthrough and take a step forward. Oh, how are the cures doing?"

Belle speaks up, "I feel great so far, Doc. Not sure how long it's supposed to take, but I think I feel a bit better already."

Zyus-Pahl raises his hand and follows her, "My skin feels elastic and strong, like it has been babied for years now."

"I can see a small change in my legs," Anna is impressed.

"I slept great last night. Mine was fast acting," Brian nods.

Igbogga shakes their head for no result.

"Glad to hear. Any further feelings or questions?" No one answers, so he continues, "Alright, let's move on. To the next universe."

Calvin and Belle hit a button or two and join pods. Nurse Goode calls them out, "Looks like we have a connection, Doctor."

Whee-Pahl looks at Anna and they both smile, then Nurse Goode smiles as well.

"Excellent! Good luck you two."

Calvin and Belle descend together, and the rest do as well. Maybe a chuckle or two echo down as they arrive in the lower half, now double what they were used to before.

Dr. Silver concedes, "I guess we'll take another break here before we continue with the next stop."

Down below, the new couple look around in the double sized cabin, then dive headfirst into each other.

Calvin whispers, "I have waited for so long to be with someone like you."

"Someone like me?'

"Yeah, vulnerable. I feel an open trust, it's weird."

"Me too, Calvin. Why don't we talk later, though."

Chapter 11: Creators- Rolling Worlds of Harmony

Where physical laws mystify and the improbable life that came about despite them, this realm is an optical illusion, and the illusion is a defense of its design. Galaxies and stars repeat themselves into an echo, and then they're gone.

Colors make sense and senses make more color, molding shapes and formations, growing in a similar fashion to fractals. Black holes multiply and emerge to concentrate and swallow stars to become accretion disks in haste. Lights flash at random moments in space, sometimes giving way to a ship of explorers.

Planets spin and birth infinite stairways, hallways, and gateways that repeat on and on, then return into a single threshold or pathway. Life appears unfazed by the confusion, so beautiful and overcomplicated, whose effects may be just for an observer's eyes. Or their true worth lies deep within the local communities, whose projections have multiple origins and purposes.

Along the outer limits of the turbulent visuals, the IAV slips through a cut in space. The craft travels with those limits until it turns inward to match the changing stars and galaxies.

The passengers finish their drinks and put the trays back into the dashboards. Calvin and Belle return to make the group complete. "Excellent. Now that we're all here, I'll start by telling you about this new universe, The Rolling Worlds of Harmony, which is the last of the Creator series of our tour of universes. This universe is the creation of an artist born at the end of the 19th century on Planet Earth, MC Escher."

"That is far out. I had a hunch when we arrived, but this is cool. I always found his artwork soothing and like it was, um, I don't know. Oh, it's the complexity that seems to drown out my pain. Oh my God, I can really feel. I'm sorry can I explain?" Anna is opening to the group.

"Of course, Anna. Continue," Dr. Silver urges her.

"Thank you. I can feel how my past relationships, I mean, I was bending over backwards, and they were taking advantage of it. All that time, it was such a deep, passive mode they exploited. I guess I was easy to exploit, but wow." Anna starts to cry, so Belle and Calvin comfort her by grabbing her arm. She dries up and sits calmly.

"Incredible breakthrough, Anna! I won't ask any questions of you right now, but I'm so happy to see you make strides," Dr. Silver and Nurse Goode smile at each other.

The nurse adds, "Keep that power within yourself, so that you know those tricks and others won't fool you again."

"Yes, thank you, both."

The group smiles at the woman in her new suit of inner strength as shapes unwind outside their vessel.

The doctor continues, "Now, some of you may have noticed that this and the two universes prior were of Human origin. So, it is the intention to give the opportunity to the Gurrs and the Zor-ahns for not having had a Creator yet."

The Gurrs smile and hold each other. The Zor-ahns stay silent for a moment, then Whee-Pahl speaks up, "It would be a great honor, and we'd do right by any gift."

"I am glad to hear you say that Whee-Pahl, and I would have easily assumed you and Zyus-Pahl would be open to the possibility."

"As long as the life forms have a chance at true good health, mental and physical, I will cherish it," Igbogga says and holds hands with Allegga.

Calvin smiles and says, "MC Escher was a certified genius, and every piece of his art I've ever seen inspired a belief in myself that I could create my own completely original and magnificent thing. I occasionally write poetry but not saying I write poetry like MC Escher draws and paints," Calvin laughs.

"I'm sure it's good. You have to let me read it," Belle puts a light slap on his forearm.

"Of course. I have plenty to write about now," Calvin nods in confidence. "I will say that this universe confuses my brain, so I have to turn away quickly."

Dr. Silver continues, "The unfolding designs are only hard on the eyes for a little bit. We'll go right through the mazes and phenomenon to some star systems that foster interesting life. All this magic is aware, and not to be interfered with, so we'll cruise around. I want to impress how the spark of creation that resided within these Creators when they were artists living mortal lives, also lives within all life forms. It is such an individual and special thing that it is different in every single life form in every existence."

"This doesn't seem like a large universe, when you compare it to others," Brian observes the realm with a countable number of galaxies. "Like 50 or 80 galaxies?"

"How do you count all of them? They are constantly echoing all around," Allegga asks Brian.

"Wait until the echoing resets and they are still for a moment. It's just an estimate."

"SOO, do you have a number for us?" Dr. Silver turns to the orb.

"Indeed, Doctor. There are 90 galaxies, and millions of worlds that support evolving life," SOO smiles. "There are no Super Beings here because all life was created here with extraordinary intelligence, so they are unnecessary. There are less species overall per planet, but all beings live with the ability to travel throughout their higher dimensions. Eating does not exist, as well as other functions of life you would find in other universes."

"How do they sustain themselves then?" Brian is curious.

SOO looks at Brian and replies, "These life forms get their energy from the light of the stars and the respiration of their planet's gases, a symbiotic trade with the local flora."

Calvin responds, "Sounds like our plants on Earth."

"Yes, very much so," Dr. Silver confirms.

"Very efficient life, huh?" Belle adds.

They enter a galaxy of swirling and protruding light, repetition and shadows, then shoot to a star system throwing ghostlike trails around them. The craft descends through the atmosphere of a planet with a mysterious movement all about the surface.

As they approach land, the travelers are perplexed and anxious at the coming projections from below. Stairways and archways and paths of different origins come together, and then apart to reconnect upside down and over there. Beneath the sprawling designs, a group of people, united in a circle, project an illusion of confusion to the travelers.

"Do any species travel in space?" Calvin asks.

SOO looks at Dr. Silver, who gestures for it to answer, and it continues, "Yes, space travel exists, but many evolved peoples connect telepathically across the stars. Some folks have ships and vessels to explore but it is mainly to monitor the cosmos here. The Creator of this universe has created a gray area where the life forms can connect to Him and see us in this IAV. They know we're here, but we're not a threat in here. Dr. Silver, I suggest we pass on by these worlds."

Staircases with handrails, and red bricks with gray wires come from a being who stands alone and projects an elegant home of confusion. Adding to the illusion, it spins out through inverted paths to combine with the already formed sections. There's no place to land anyway.

"Thank you, SOO," Dr. Silver directs the craft up and out of the climbing staircases, as the deceptive protrusions keep them at a distance.

The IAV flies over another world in the same system, which explodes in similar illusions towards the traveling craft. "Ooh!" The Gurrs hug each other and watch in amazement.

"This seems like a weird way to live a life, Dr. Silver. Do they experience 'normal living' in any way, like we all did?"

Dr. Silver turns to Calvin, "These people reproduce with pleasure, digest the starlight, and contemplate their existence. They live a grateful life of art and duty to honor their Creator."

"All worlds and all people live life like this. Do any stray?" Anna asks.

"Yes, and we'll go there after we see the rest of this system. Did anyone notice how the illusions of the people on the planet we visited first were like the patterns of this one here we're passing?" Dr. Silver asks the group.

"What does that mean?" Anna asks him. "I'm curious."

"They are all connected and think those illusions are how to repel us?" Belle asks.

"Well, yes, but as SOO told us earlier, their connection is direct to the Creator once known as MC Escher, so their manifestations are a derivative of this lord," Dr. Silver explains.

The IAV shoots out of the star system, whose people's echoing illusions were a wall to the outsiders, and makes its way to a new galaxy that shows no sign of an echo or multiplying star. They zoom through dust and gas, to a system of twelve planets.

"We'll stop into this one first." The doctor continues, "You'll see the disarray, it is quite apparent."

The craft moves down toward the surface and makes it to 30 feet or so off the plush landscape of green and pink colors. People of a hominid species try to interact with each other but argue and project illusions at each other. Some are afraid and run, while others team to surround the tussle and create a bubble of replicating stairs and pathways.

"These people are so chaotic," Calvin says.

"Do they seem familiar?" Dr. Silver says to him.

"They seem like Earthlings to me," Calvin says and Belle nods. She looks at Anna, who takes a moment and agrees.

"Yes, these folks resemble Humans, in a few ways, with so many gifts and no consideration for others. The other star system, with the proper echoes and illusions, was what the Gurrs' world is like, in a matter of speaking." Dr. Silver continues, "Zor-ahns— such a peaceful world with so wise a people, well, I don't think anyone here resembles you guys."

"That is an interesting assessment of our world, Dr. Silver. I didn't realize my people were capable of more technology, because we have more than we need," Zyus-Pahl replies.

The IAV travels over changing landscapes and random bouts of chaos bloom to decorate the surface. Nurse Goode sees something on her tablet, "Dr. Silver, we can go see him now if you wish."

Dr. Silver looks around and smiles, "We will now go see the Creator of this universe."

They shoot out of the star system and out of the galaxy, past other galaxies that echo and multiply, and come to the artist himself, MC Escher. Infinite designs and shapes surround the craft and dazzle the travelers. The deity smiles at them.

Suddenly, the IAV is in a multiple, mirrored reality with various illusions! Madness surrounds them, and even Brian is a touch scared. He regains his composure and looks around at his fellow travelers, including the smiling doctor. Then, the nauseating illusion breaks apart and backs together as the great being resumes the illusions with another smile.

"I think he likes us," Dr. Silver assumes.

"Anybody else a little out of their mind by this? I mean, he is amazing but the situation here is unbelievable," Calvin is excited. "Wow, Dr. Silver, I'm used to being excited and scared of becoming manic when something good or fun happens, but I feel so... At peace."

"Excellent, Calvin."

"There were some cool facts about this universe. My favorite is that they don't eat food," Belle says, which draws a smile from Calvin.

"Truly, Belle. Never feeling hungry, they probably don't think much about it. Any other thoughts on this incredible place?" Dr. Silver says as the illusions create a pocket of heaven around them that it becomes a day at the beach with clear, blue waters.

With some sounds of ease, the group goes silent. Anna exhales with a powerful push, and adds more breathing in, "When we look deep inside at our individual attributes, and recognize we are all unique, we can truly feel free on the outside."

"Ooh, yes. Good one, Anna," Dr. Silver smiles at her with a nod.

"What about feeling lonely from time to time? I feel like I would be lonely as a Creator," Allegga says to the others.

Zyus-Pahl shakes his head, "I would only do this if Whee were with me."

"That will be part of your options. Our journey continues with a place you may all see as place to settle for richer and healthier lives, but I'll tell you more when we arrive." Dr. Silver looks at his tablet and continues, "Let's pick back up with revelations from our trip. We've had a breakthrough with Anna, which was really something, and Calvin continued to make progress. Anybody want to add anything?"

Brian speaks up, "I see now how different types of people can make different types of existences for themselves and those around them. I kind of feel something for the people in the various universes who suffer or are held to a seemingly lower standard of life than I was, but so much that I understand and know is based on years of experience, good and bad. They may have put themselves in those places by being cruel. I have opinions, but I'm not killing people."

Calvin replies, "No one ever said you can't have opinions, but when you are antagonistic and apathetic, I will argue and defend myself. I've had plenty of experience around people like you." He opens his eyes wider, and they stare at each other for a few seconds.

"I would like to say something else," Anna jumps into the discussion.

Dr. Silver gestures to her, "Of course, go on."

"Something just dawned on me— I never have to live with the type of manipulation and shame of my past anymore. I can see myself being whole and without fear of others' reactions to me. Confidence now runs through me, and I feel like the good person I used to feel like when I was unaware of those evils of Humanity. I can let go of the past, especially since I won't see those men again," Anna looks outside and stares at a small wave coming ashore.

"That was spectacular, Anna! And, Brian, time will tell. Okay, we've been to a few planets where there was harmony among the population, and one planet, not so much. Harmony comes about when most everyone develops full compassion and consideration."

There is a comfortable silence, and it's not broken until the blue beach heaven dissolves before them. A few gasps as some geometric anomalies sprout to confuse them, then the deity vanishes.

Dr. Silver goes on, "Excellent. I now want to tell you all, as we move on to the next universe, to keep those minds open." The IAV blasts beyond the rest of the illusions, to the edge of the realm, then slips through a crevice tucked in an echo...

Chapter 12: Dynamic Universe

In a vast expanse, galaxies of all shapes and orientations glide and avoid each other as if choreographed to do so. Streams of light travel alone, and in groups, with no fire or burn to them. Black holes are black holes, with most of the massive ones in the center of galaxies, but streams of light spin around them as they engulf small and medium stars caught in their grasp.

Planets orbit healthy stars with wide habitable zones that can support multiple life-bearing worlds. With an abundance of species throughout this cosmos, sufficient technology, comradery, and love are common. Certain spacemen fly around the larger structures and tend to the construction and maintenance, while others do so in an apparent joy.

In a dark corner of the large universe, the IAV explodes into the new realm with a blast of sparkling shards. As it comes to a rest, the folks look to the new place with enthusiasm. Those who can feel joy in the moment, anyway. Inside, Dr. Silver looks up from his tablet and controls to the craft, "Ah, yes, welcome to the Dynamic Universe, as it is called. Here all spirits within can be reincarnated to a chosen life form after death and stay here in this expanse to find their love again. Loved ones can reunite here. You start new lives but remember past lives and the times had together."

"Does our universe do this?" Calvin asks.

"Not quite, Calvin. Your universe has the chance to reincarnate to the same world, but spirits usually go to a new world and family. Spirits can end up in new universes, as we've covered. Here is where many travelers, like you, have chosen to stay," Dr. Silver says to him as he directs the craft to fly into a galaxy nearby. "I want to show you all what happens here when a star dies. Compared to how it would die in your universe, here it happens a bit differently."

They travel to a lonesome star in space, one that seems content to burn alone without a planet to feed. Flares and flames scold and keep calm the energy around. Several streams of light, from various origins, fly by the IAV.

"What are those things of light?" Anna asks as she points to an illuminated trail.

"Those are said to be the spirits on their travels after life. Maybe to go around space and come back to be with their loved ones again."

"This is really cool, Igbogga," Allegga says to their partner. "Want to stay?"

"I think I'd be fine here, but I might rather stay for the whole tour," Igbogga replies.

Allegga hugs them, and says, "I'm with you."

The star burns steadily for a few minutes, which makes the travelers a bit restless. Dr. Silver breaks the silence, "Shouldn't be too much longer." Then, it burns a thousand times brighter and collapses down into itself. As it shrinks into nothing, a bright light shines and expands instantly to become the same burner as before.

Everyone gasps and nods, then they look around at each other. Dr. Silver smiles, "Cool, right? Now, let's look at an advanced species. I promise this won't disappoint either." The IAV leaves the star behind, and shoots across the universe.

"Does this mean entropy does not exist either?" Brian wonders.

"Yes, Brian. Stars never die unless they get sucked into the black holes, but the stars will continue to emerge in the far reaches of this deep space."

They pass many star systems and slow to a viewing velocity in the vicinity of a planet, to orbit a star with a large space structure. The fabrication houses a fleet of spaceships, all primed for launch, and countless panels to absorb energy from the star. The world is lit on the dark side with the designs of people not burdened by overpopulation but a preference for the optimization of all things.

"A Dyson sphere, right?" Brian asks.

"Uh, yes," Dr. Silver answers. "These people are among the most advanced and have plenty of space to explore. The spirits that explore space in life continue to do so in subsequent lives too. The people who develop into artists and scientists and explorers do so in each life they live and sometimes become known for their acknowledged string of lives. Let's look at the surface."

The craft flies through a bit of traffic in orbit and begins its descent. As they pierce the light clouds, a view through the blue sky of a landscape of great architectural structures draws them near an open park with few trees. With a smooth descent, the IAV lands without a bump. Allegga and Igbogga smile. They all smile at the beautiful city with its peaceful people.

Dr. Silver leads them out of the craft and turns to them, "We can mingle with these people. They are more advanced than any of you here and many here are from the same travels as you. This building here has a gathering worth witnessing." He points to a large building across the brick lane from the park.

The group leaves the bubble, and they all notice the same thing, but Calvin says it first, "This air unbelievable! It is so pure, anybody else?"

The others agree with nods, and even Zyus-Pahl perks up, "It is just delightful. It may already be clearing up my upper sinuses." He inhales through his nose and Whee-Pahl joins him in the fresh air. "My skin has cleared up, Dr. Silver. All the little cuts have closed. Between the IAV and this place, Whee, I almost forget how bad dry skin feels.

"So, there's not enough people to create any pollution?" Calvin asks. "What about waste?"

"You are correct about pollution. I'm not sure about waste, let's try to remember to ask SOO when we return," Dr. Silver replies as they walk to the brick lane and the Zor-ahns try to keep up. "Oh, and to anyone who wishes to remain in the Dynamic Universe, there are other planets with different levels of technology, ones where people live simpler and maybe more in tune with nature." He looks at the building with tall columns and continues, "Let's go in here."

They walk across the street to the sidewalk. Few pedestrians populate the town, but occasional carpools and odd couples deliver sounds of bliss. Traffic is so light, one vehicle slows down early to let them pass. The building is made of a pink concrete looking material, which is a sight for the travelers. They take a moment and stare all around.

Up the stairs, they follow the doctor to a large set of red doors. As they swing open with some weight to them, the clean floors shine perfectly. There is no one inside the entrance, and no one in the silent halls to overcome Brian's voice, "No one here?"

Dr. Silver whispers, "Through these doors here, but be quiet." They all look at Brian and he shrugs.

They go through the doors into the grand foyer, which is a spacious area lined with flags bookending multiple banquet rooms. One room has a door cracked and some voices echo into the hallway. The travelers go inside and join a group of around twenty people of different species in what appears to be an official gathering.

They all greet the strangers with smiles. One fellow in the middle of the room, with a smooth, tan complexion and big ears, welcomes them, "Hello, strangers. I am Ellard, and this is the council of Planet Well. Please come in and join our discussion."

Dr. Silver steps up and responds, "Hi Ellard, I am Dr. Silver. You may have a couple from our group." He turns to his eight passengers behind him, "Do any of you wish to become free spirits in this world or stay on your journey?"

Allegga looks at their partner, "We thought about it, can we decide later to come back here?"

Dr. Silver smiles at them, "Of course you can. You can all decide at the very end of the tour what you wish to do. It is a major decision. Ellard, we may return to Planet Well. Would that be acceptable?"

Ellard smiles, "Absolutely. We don't have problems of overpopulation, so we never need anything. We're grateful to live in this existence and we honor God by welcoming all travelers as our own. People of all kinds and orientations remain with us. We have it pretty good here. Our disagreements are usually handled in the moment because things are just. Not desperate."

Igbogga speaks up, "Let's remember this one, Allegga. It's ideal. Let's keep this one at the top."

"I agree."

Ellard asks them, "What type of life and existence to do you want to live? Do you want to live a mortal life and be reborn with the comfort of the loves you build in this paradise, or maybe another pleases you. And the choice to become a Creator is one with which many in this place are familiar. Would the visitors like to join our discussion over a mid-day meal?"

Calvin brightens up, "I could eat something. Belle, can you eat the food here?"

"I'm supposedly healing with the medicine, but I'll still remain within my limits," Belle is game.

"Okay then. You people can come with us, and we'll introduce you to some other residents. We take time every few days to celebrate our world and serene lives. Together, we share a powerful love, and the community thrives as a result," Ellard waves them along with the local crowd.

Lights go on in a large banquet hall adorned with many shapes of white flowers and white linens and sashes. The windows, along the middle section of the high ceilings, are both transparent and artistic. Cutlery, of a metal similar looking to platinum, are bundled with each place setting.

"Welcome to our banquet hall, and the best food in the province," Ellard smiles with his fellow people from Well. As they take seats, the food is brought to the tables and placed in the middle for self-service. As they get ready to eat, he continues, "Does anyone want to say the blessing? One of our visitors would be welcome to speak of their gratitudes or dreams as well."

The eight travelers look at each other, but a couple side glances in Brian's direction make Calvin giggle, which looks to have embarrassed Dr. Silver, who says, "Uh, Calvin, would you like to say something profound for us? Our friend here is a poet and has some real deep thoughts." He looks at Calvin, now biting a side of his bottom lip.

Calvin looks at Dr. Silver as though they all got him in the gag, "Okay, okay. I got this. I think." He then looks at Belle, who smiles back with unwavering energy, and prays, "Dear Lord God, please bless all who eat among us, prepare our meals, and grow the ingredients. Please help all spirits, lost in existence, find a new, beautiful life in a universe that is as wonderful as this Planet Well. We are grateful and now we enjoy the moment together."

Everyone smiles with delight, "Amen."

Calvin and Belle, who sit next to each other and stay inside their own attention bubble, serve each other from the platters. The meat is carved into slices and looks like turkey. Other sides, two colors of pudding, a bread stuffing like side dish, and various fruits, not completely unlike those from Earth, are among the unusual fare.

There is a low chatter when Calvin speaks up, "What kind of animal is this we are eating?" The other Humans look at Ellard as they think about what they are about to eat."

Ellard replies, "We manufacture this meat to cater to every one of us. It is rich in nutrients and protein, without the things that clog veins and stop hearts. Taste it, you'll like it. We have all kinds of sauces." He points to a tray of sauces in the middle of the table near Calvin. "Yeah, right there. The tray."

Belle grabs the sauces and the Humans all try their mystery meat...

Dr. Silver waves to the assembly, "Thank you everyone! We'll be on our way now."

Ellard stands and waves to them, "It was a great pleasure to spend this meal with all of you. Calvin, thank you for your words."

With waves and goodbyes, there are a lot of honest smiles plus one stoic with baseline manners. The energy lifts both groups as the travelers depart.

Fresh air wafts inside as they pull the doors open. "Man, that air!" Anna exclaims as they exit the building. "I was thinking of staying here but it's not like I have anyone to be reborn with, so."

"It seems a bit boring to me. They explore space by going to other worlds that are populated by beings from these tours," Calvin acts agitated.

"Is there an issue, Calvin?" Dr. Silver asks him.

"Yes, kind of, Dr. Silver. My mind is twitchy and feel like my skin is crawling with insects. Very uneasy and agitated. No one said anything or did anything, it may be the meat we ate." He starts to lose focus and his balance a bit, but Dr. Silver and Belle each take a side.

"Okay, stay with me as we get back to the IAV," Dr. Silver guides Calvin with Belle's help.

They cross the road with a pace still fast enough that they leave behind the Zor-ahns. After Zyus-Pahl huffs, the smaller couple keeps up with a fast trot.

"I mean, the meat tasted good. The sauces, they were like a weird BBQ, and creamy like ranch or." Calvin struggles while he is helped along the path.

"Yeah, they were good," Belle says to him. She looks at Brian, "Can you help him for me, please?"

Brian shrugs it off, "We're almost there, Belle. You got it. He didn't have to eat that food. None of us did."

Belle asks the doctor, "Why was he the only Human to get sick?"

Dr. Silver replies, "It must be his medicine." He and Belle get Calvin to the IAV after a minute of silence and sit Calvin down on a step. He turns around, "Does anyone have anything to add?"

Whee-Pahl speaks up first, "This was a wonderful world, and I am so happy we were able to meet those nice people."

Dr. Silver replies to her, "Yes, Whee-Pahl, it was very nice, I agree."

Calvin feels his stomach, and looks at Belle, "My stomach doesn't feel that well. I'm sorry for what you must go through, Belle. The stomach is such an awful place to have pain." He gets up and gathers himself enough to board the vessel.

The rest of the travelers board the craft and take their seats. They lift off the ground into the blue sky, passing by flying astronauts, as they become invisible and enter the black of space. There isn't a word.

The IAV shoots toward another planet in another system, but here, there are no explorers. It is peaceful, and the planet has some lights here and there on the surface. They descend through some cloud cover to a paradise of nature, colors and textures that puzzle the eyes.

"We'll just set down over here in this bare piece of grass." Dr. Silver brings the craft to a stop on the ground and turns to them, "Folks, here's a place I want to show you that is just perfect. Perfection of life and landscape— just a treat. We can discuss our travels and issues here, as there are no other people."

Nurse Goode says, "We can bring SOO outside as well, and I have a portable maker for drinks."

They all exit the vehicle to an overload of fresh air and flowers everywhere. Each explorer takes a moment as they walk to an open area in the flowers to a circle of seats with a bar. Each one has a drink, and they all sit and take in the beauty.

Dr. Silver nods, "Everyone comfortable? I want to go around the circle, but no one is required to talk, as usual. How about, Zyus-Pahl?"

Zyus-Pahl sits up and clears his throat, "Thank you, Doctor. I have expanded my awareness with all of you, if nothing else, and find it difficult to imagine a life now without my new friends who also know the depths of this profound experience."

Whee-Pahl nods and speaks up, "I agree. When we left for the first time, we both feared never seeing you nice people again. We enjoyed this experience greatly, and I also realized that since I am traveling with Zyus, my Carpal Tunnel Syndrome feels like it is easing and feeling is returning to my hands. I was overusing them, but I had no choice at home."

Calvin agrees, "First, I think that food was a little off for me. It must be my medicine, right? Well, no big deal. I'm with Zyus-Pahl, it's hard to lose a friend when you been through so much with them."

Allegga adds, "What a beautiful world of peaceful people. There are many wonderful places as much as the terrifying ones."

"It was sad when we thought Zyus-Pahl and Whee-Pahl left us, so I'm grateful they're back. I value each of you and it has been fun to learn with you," Belle says in her sweet Southern accent.

Dr. Silver chimes in, "And we aren't done yet either. We have just three universes left before we take the final leg of the tour, beyond this current existence called the Space Time Dimensional Construct. The tour will end in a special Universe, back inside the construct, where your decisions can be made."

There is a moment of silence as they all enjoy the environment with deep breaths and sips from their glasses. Butterflies and bees and all kinds of insects move about and adorn the scenery. Small animals fritter and search without hesitation.

Dr. Silver stands up and stretches, "Let's move on, shall we?"

No arguments as they get up and stretch and shake out the willies, then they make their way back onto the IAV.

The peaceful land remains as it was, and the craft lifts off into space. As they travel out of the system, their path out of the galaxy goes through a large spaceship. Flashes of local passengers going to a distant place make the group smile.

They pass all the galaxies at great speeds, and no one speaks, then shoot out of the edge of the universe through a small hole in space...

Chapter 13: No Matter Universe

Nothing. There is only deep space of unmeasurable size, this universe lacks celestial objects, and for that matter, any real mass. Gas clouds would hint at bigger things, but they cannot be found. Random waves of energy, maybe from beyond, travel through the darkness together, and then apart. Many dots of light, small and bright, gather and spread apart and dance through this permanent night.

Hints of noise reverberate together with a layer of penetrating voices to leave nothing behind in the emptiness. Rolls of laughter and whimpers of sorrow smother each other, and a booming, lower one silences them into submission. Giggles and more giggles, with great laughter, are again silenced by that lower voice. Phantom galaxies and stars appear and flourish with illuminated centers, only to explode and dissipate across the cosmos.

Another spot of light in the darkness welcomes the IAV to this universe. It flies about, but through and around nothing. Dr. Silver brings it to stop and turns to the group, "Alrighty, all of you back up and rested and good?" They nod. "This trip is quite long, but as long as we end up where we really belong, that's what's important, right?"

Calvin jokes, "Sometimes a trip to where we don't belong can be fun, right? A little trouble can be fun. Woo-hoo!" His energy is tense.

Anna shakes her head, "No, thank you. I'm good with staying where I belong."

"Fun can be fun, but what if where you belong is fun?" Belle asks him.

"That is true, Belle. I agree overall, Doctor, but wait. What was I talking about? So, where are we?" Calvin's enthusiasm shines beyond his bright smile, to cross into mania.

Dr. Silver types something on his tablet. He looks over to Calvin, "Hey Calvin, please read my message."

Calvin opens his tablet then points down to Belle as he goes below, "I'll be a minute, Belle." She smiles and returns her attention to the group.

"Let's wait for Calvin to return. He won't be long," Dr. Silver pauses a moment.

Calvin drops into his little room that is now much bigger inside. He grabs his pills off the nightstand and walks to the bathroom to fill a glass of water, "I'm about to float on clouds of pillows and land slowly on the ground." He breathes and wipes his eyes, then pours the ones from the section marked 'Th AM' into his mouth with the water.

He puts his head back and closes his eyes as he lets his head touch the wall. He sips the water a few times, "Mmm. I think I'll lie down a minute." Calvin rests on his bed for a few moments...

The group talk is about foods and drinks of their worlds as Calvin pops back up to them. He and Belle share a smile.

"Hey, there he is! We all good to go, Mr. Wayne?" Dr. Silver is gentle in tone.

Calvin smiles, "Yes sir, Doctor! Thanks for helping me make a correction."

"Glad to help. I am glad you're back, Calvin. It hurts to watch someone suffer like that. I've seen many forms of it." Dr. Silver looks outside the IAV and his lights go on, "Oh yes, so I want you all to look outside the canopy to see the vast darkness of the No Matter Universe or the Open Universe. These are where universes begin and develop into realms that flourish and are abundant with cosmic turmoil and sacred life."

"So, this place is just empty?" Brian asks and is already uninterested.

"Brian, this place is without mass, but you'll find it is definitely not empty," Dr. Silver looks back outside and points to a cloud that approaches them. He hits the controls and they shoot through a wave of green light. As they close in on it, the cloud reveals itself as a cluster of lights. Maybe they are even described as orbs.

"What is that?" Brian changes his tune.

The lights surround the IAV, and random voices sing or talk around them. Some are sad and depressing in tone, but others are surely brave or just joyful. A few are curious and some without much awareness to make up a following of agreeable ones.

"This is what it looks like in the beginning of a universe. These are spirits ready to find and become life forms, but it is a long wait, so they search. Did you notice anything specific about the spirits? Anyone?" Dr. Silver asks them.

Belle looks around and replies, "I heard different emotions and what seemed like voices."

"Yes, because these spirits are individuals. We bring ourselves from life to life. Some are Primary spirits, but most are normal, reincarnating souls. There may be other things, though, as we've seen."

Some of the spirits gather around Brian's pod, and the other travelers look over. He puts his hand on the canopy where a few of them dance along the outline of his fingers. One figure moves directly in front of his face, and a few others follow but make a circle around the one.

Brian moves his head and the lights dance with him. He then jumps to make them flinch and laughs at them. "Oh my God, the lights are kind of sad out there, no one to help them, just flying around," he says, and swipes at their mutual line of sight, prompting the group of lights to turn from pink to red to burgundy. They all fly away together.

Dr. Silver is not pleased and interrupts, "Brian, these spirits have feelings, and there are significant dangers. I hope Aurfuud doesn't mind that incident."

As Dr. Silver finishes his warning, an apparition with a dizzying number of random faces appears in the darkness ahead. As it gets near, a body of light emerges underneath, and the faces coalesce around a grave, blue face with a red mouth. The discernible visage speaks, "Who is the offender?"

"The Demon of a Thousand Faces! It's Aurfuud!" Dr. Silver looks at Brian and the others.

Calvin grabs Belle, "Don't look at it, Belle. Don't look."

Igbogga freaks out, "Oh my, oh my, oh my!"

Allegga comforts Igbogga, "We're together, just hold on."

It says again, "Bring me the offender. You will come with me to meet your fate. Your transgression, the ridicule of a Primary Spirit, to be judged now."

Brian's eyes are wide as a bubble of light grabs him from the group, and they disappear!

Dr. Silver looks at Nurse Goode and whispers, "We have to prepare for everything."

She agrees, "Yes, Doctor."

Brian wakes up in the bubble of light, within the swirling, uncountable faces that all stare at him. He can see small flashes outside their grasp and mumbles to himself, "Where the Hell are we going?"

Aurfuud responds through each face's mouth and expressions, "Almost there, life form."

A window, through the faces, exposes an expanse like nothing he's ever seen before, with a mesmerizing pattern of proportion his mind doesn't really process. Brian tries to think but can only squint hard. He asks, "Please let me go back to the group. I didn't mean to hurt their feelings."

"Yes. You. Did."

Before Brian can answer the Demon, he is thrown into a new kind of darkness. One of solitude with the echoes of a slow drip. Some boulders sit on the desolate ground. Sadness and hopelessness take over, "Is what I did really that bad? This place is too scary; I must keep positive."

As Brian sits on a boulder, he sees a beast like an over-sized wolf with lit up, white eyes. It approaches him and speaks, "I am the conjuring of Darkness, in the Great Void. Brian Harper of Earth, you have sinned a great sin and shall pay with your spirit. Only self-sacrifice can save your soul. You will be given the ability to bring others into your despair. The best moment to bring them down will be in the Reflection. Your only way out of this appears to be a path you are unwilling to travel."

Brian feels nothing as he finds himself within a light bubble, traveling at a speed like the IAV.

Millions of lights, all the eager spirits, arrive and surround the giant spark. No sounds, just different brightnesses. Another phenomenon streaks from far away to the group. It looks familiar to Anna, "Is that Aurfuud again?"

Dr. Silver joins the others in the observation, "I believe so, Anna. Let's see if Brian has come back as a changed man, and ready to be considerate."

It is Aurfuud, and as quickly as it arrived, it is now gone and Brian is back in the IAV with the others. Brian looks at everyone with a quiet nod, then descends to his private area.

"I wonder what is going on there, huh?" Calvin asks.

"I wonder too, Calvin, but I know he is alone for a good reason. Let's continue with the journey, and he will return when he is ready." Dr. Silver adds, "As I was saying, or going to say, this universe has a new Creator, and it will take shape over time. The gases gather and form clouds, debris clumps into rock and substance."

The universe follows his words and stars appear all around. Small, young stars in a young universe. The travelers gaze upon the lights and collisions.

"This is wild, isn't it?" Calvin says.

"Totally awesome," Belle smiles as she grabs Calvin's arm.

Brian returns to the group with a new air of confidence, like nothing happened. The others give slight glances with no real way to connect.

"Um, one moment everyone. Brian, are you okay and ready to move on?" Dr. Silver asks and gets a nod from Brian. "Yes, okay, let's watch these stellar formations and discuss our next hurdle together, which is dealing with someone who is having a difficult time."

A cloud of colorful dust and gas grows throughout the center of the universe, and more explosions and collisions occur as time is accelerated. More stars are born, and rocky planets and gas giants appear near them. The greater stars become black holes that draw in star systems and gas clouds closer, to create spiraling galaxies.

"I wonder what it feels like to heal completely from my illnesses and start a universe. Think of all the awesome details that would influence all of life and physics for its eternity," Calvin ponders.

"You would love the freedom, I'm sure. As would anyone with a serious illness," Dr. Silver says.

"This is all so incredible," Calvin looks outside and sees some lights dance in the distance.

Dr. Silver looks at Brian again, and asks him, "Brian, I apologize if I am too pushy, but do you wish to add anything to our discussion? We saw the birth of a universe and some Primary Spirits before that. Did they scare you straight?"

Brian looks at Calvin in a new, drier way, then to the doctor, "I was always straight. Please! I feel better now than before."

Anna is unconvinced, "Brian, what happened to you out there? Where did that thing bring you?"

Brian doesn't keep eye contact with her, "Somewhere scary and bad. I hope I never go back, and I think. I feel like it was mostly a vision to scare me. There are places out there that you had better stay happy and not give in to sadness and hopelessness. Don't go down that road even a little. Calvin, I feel bad for you- you can't help it. You must feel like you have one foot in the door to the Darkness."

A quick moment of silent contemplation, then a few of them grab drinks. Calvin gets close to Belle.

"What's next, Doc?" Belle asks him.

"Well, I guess we're all done here. We are, right?" A short pause and Dr. Silver go on, "Let's move on to the next universe, which is one of my favorites."

The IAV zooms in toward the growing cosmos and then shoots out of the other end, through a small sliver of black...

PART THREE

Chapter 14: Universe of the Little Universes

Proportions of preposterous design, exponentially felt and observed by those few who live within. Origins of imagination and its ability to connect life to Creation, this is the fountain of inspiration. Honest, unconditional love is returned, which enables the cycle to continue.

In significant passing moments, time is a constant so the super-beings can share a reality. Life exists in different scales and within these exalted deities who dwell and ponder their populations inside. Life, here and in every universe, is also connected by the imaginations of the ones brave enough to dream.

A single star system is an entire universe, with nine worlds in their own elliptical orbits around a great ball of fire. Four are gas giants, and the rest are solid rock and ore, mostly. Three belts of asteroids and gas try to isolate parts of the lone system, if it were possible to keep these great beings isolated.

In an inner section of belts, one rock and ore world does not draw energy or resources but IS a source of energy, where this life is not what it seems.

At the edge of the star system, a small dot of light gives way to an emerging IAV. The vessel shoots through the outer belt and then the middle belt, to join the special planet in this awesome view. "I want to welcome you to the Universe of the Little Universes. This one is different, friends. I guess, they're all different in some way, like all of us," Dr. Silver looks at Brian and Calvin.

The IAV flies close enough in orbit to reveal clouds interlaced with orbs and planks that glow white or blue to form an intricate network. A being of a different nature peaks up from the maze of wonder and grabs the IAV, with a gentle force, and pulls it down inside. The craft is freed and wanders to an open cloud with a view.

They get a closer look at the being, which reveals a temporal border of sorts, and an expanse within. Not flesh, nor a type of shell, or even scale, but something with a squeezed, yet vast dimension shocks all of them. A being with the outline of a hominid, but it is another realm where galaxies and celestial objects exist.

Belle is freaking out, "What is going here, Dr. Silver?"

"Yeah, this doesn't look safe to me. Look at this creature. What is it made of?" Calvin asks.

"Are those stars?" Zyus-Pahl asks.

Dr. Silver looks at him and smiles widely, "Zyus-Pahl, you said it. Those are stars and other celestial objects in their appearance. Does anyone want to guess what they are? This universe was created for a reason and proportion is not what it seems."

"Are they celestials? Or are those spirits primary spirits for their worlds?" Calvin seems like he has other possibilities in mind.

"I think they're Star Borns or something. I see a few of them over there and they are not really communicating," Anna is confused at what she sees: four of the beings gather and the lights around them begin to blind the onlookers. Then, the lights dim and the beings disperse.

"You were close, kind of. These life forms are Imagi's, like Creators but rather life forms in another universe. Each Imagi is an entire universe, living in a chosen domain where energy can flow from within them, from these other worlds inside where life endures in its own ways and means." Dr. Silver continues, "They can alter the physics in their own domains, provided it doesn't interfere outside."

Calvin is still curious, "What are the lights?"

Dr. Silver nudges SOO, "What are these lights on this world, SOO?"

"The lights both transfer and store energy for the beings to share, which helps them preserve life and hope in all of their universes," SOO explains. "The network of lights and clouds covers this world completely so that all of these universes can thrive internally."

Calvin scrunches his eyebrows, "Two things: Are they talking to one another? And what does the energy do inside their own universes?"

SOO looks at Dr. Silver and puts its hand on the doctor's knee, "I have this one, Doc. Calvin, they feel so much inside that they prefer solitude together and it seems peaceful, doesn't it? Their speech is limited with little opinion or fiction to stay in the proper vibration. And, since energy is what connects all beings to Existence and help create all life, everywhere, these beings can see us traveling. This universe has the purest and strongest flow of energy of any universe because these beings aren't just transferring energy, they harmonize it into shareable power. That power is manifested into imagination and consciousness, with the help of Dark Matter and Energy."

Each passenger takes a sip of their chosen beverage or a bite of food, and they look out of the canopy at the giants. Belle goes below, then Calvin joins her. The rest drops down. Nurse Goode jokes, "Did you pass wind?"

Dr. Silver looks at Nurse Goode, "Ha, no, but that *was* weird. I guess we're taking a small break in the middle of this tour. I thought it was going kind of well, didn't you?"

Nurse Goode responds, "Yes, my Love. Of course. Remember, this is a lot for them."

The Zor-ahns and Gurrs return to the cabin where the doctor and nurse review their tablets. Then, Brian and Anna return separately.

Anna looks around and smiles, "Oh, yeah, of course. We're waiting for those two now. I think it may be a good time to have a cocktail." The others look at her as she types on her tablet, and a drink appears in her console. "Yes sir. I'll be over here, on ice."

Dr. Silver smirks at her, "Drinks are advised at certain times. I tend to get carried away and talk a lot, so I'll refrain. But Nurse, you go ahead. Be a gal pal." He smiles at Nurse Goode.

Nurse Goode makes her own drink and sits back, so Whee-Pahl gets one of her choices, and is joined by the Gurrs. Zyus-Pahl grabs what looks like a beer, and Brian gets a water.

Calvin and Belle return to the group, a little messy. "We miss anything?" Calvin asks the doctor.

"No, Calvin. All is well. Do you and Belle need a minute to gather yourselves?" Dr. Silver asks them.

"No, we're good, why?" Belle, and her frizzy hair, speaks for both.

She takes a big breath and exhales with a smile.

"Are we going to visit another species here or is this it?" Calvin asks.

"Well, yes, but the view will spook you. Possibly," Dr. Silver turns to his console and steers the IAV towards a being.

"Doc, are we going-" Calvin goes quietly to witness it.

They lift off the cloud of comfort and approach a giant. As they come close to its exterior, the craft shrinks into a dot of light and breaches the lining's darkness, into a new dimension of warped space and time.

Galaxies speed by until they cruise into one with a full star system that hosts a strange planet. The planet is metallic and robotic, with flying and space faring vehicles in great numbers outside its orbit. The beings seem non-violent.

"This is incredible, almost like a few stories from television— a cartoon and a live action show," Calvin is in awe.

Allegga smirks, "You Humans love the cartoons!" The Humans laugh with them.

"I think I know what ones you're talking about, Space Trek, or whatever." Anna says.

Calvin disagrees, "No, it's another cartoon but it was made into movies. Conscious machines that transform from a robot to a vehicle and back. I can't remember the name for some reason."

"Wow, I can't either. I used to watch two different shows that had that. I think one had cheaper toys, but I'm a bit fuzzy," Belle ponders.

"Interesting viewpoints everybody, and they are all relevant. I want to show you all a couple more civilizations inside this one great being," Dr. Silver says with cards up his sleeve.

"I'm curious what the connection is now," Zyus-Pahl says like he was holding back.

The IAV flies out of that system and to another one close by, but in the same galaxy. This place is surrounded by its primary star and has an energy-absorbing structure. "Here, is another species who has now created a Dyson Sphere to grab as much solar power as possible. We've seen a couple of these already, I think. These people are going places, right?"

"This is a joy to watch. Isn't it, Whee?"

"It is, Zyus. I am overwhelmed by all the places we've been

already."

"Now, this is Star Trek or Wars, right?" Anna asks them.

"Yeah, this is closer to that." Calvin asks the doctor, "Do any of these advanced civilizations, in any of the places we've been, ever realize what universe they are in? I mean, look at these guys out here— do they know they are part of such a spectacular being?"

"I doubt it. Maybe some random life form in a universe or two, here or there, can see Existence for what it is. and what it isn't," Dr. Silver turns back to the controls and moves the craft around the ships and stations.

The craft flies through the Dyson Sphere and the yellow star, then shoots to a binary star system with many planets and moons. One belt of rocks and asteroids sits toward the outer edge of the bubble, and the two stars seem small.

As they approach, ships cruise around, as well as individuals without visible propulsion. Zyus-Pahl doesn't understand, "Is there a reason they can fly around in this star system?"

Dr. Silver replies, "SOO, what is the story here?"

"These people can fly around here because the concepts that make up life can change from star to star. Some planets have exceptionally intelligent life and others have different physics. I'll be here all night."

"I suppose we have learned enough that I should be more intuitive by now." Dr. Silver throws up his hands.

Calvin jumps in, "I think I know what Zyus-Pahl is getting at. Do they breathe? Do they have lighter gravity?"

SOO smiles, "Ah, I'm just messing around, you guys. I was getting a little bored here. These people have breathable air throughout the entire system and gravity is gridlocked with the surplus of planets and moons."

Dr. Silver adds, "Now, has anyone figured out the connection of these three planets I showed you? Hint: remember what your guesses were about."

Anna thinks she knows, "They were all television shows or something?"

"Close."

Calvin guesses, "Dr. Silver said something about their power being manifested in imagination."

"You're on the right path, Calvin," the doctor wants him to figure it out.

Everyone is stumped, then Belle answers, "Are all stories and arts, that are not based in reality, directly inspired by these realities?"

"That is correct, Belle! Excellent work everyone! Now, let's move on from these systems and exit this Imagi," Dr. Silver says as he reclines his chair.

The IAV shoots out of the binary system and speeds to the border of the Imagi, whose hand reaches inside and escorts the craft out onto a blue, lighted orb. "Now, we're on an energy orb, and we're fine for a moment."

"These guys are awesome, full of wonder," Belle smiles and then looks at Calvin. He holds her hand.

"This place is totally trippy, by the way," Calvin smiles back at her and then looks at Dr. Silver. "I feel at ease here, Doc. It just seems like a good balance has been found here."

"Yes, it is that. Does this place stir any other feelings? Anyone?"

"It took me a moment to gather this thought, but what I am seeing and have been through has been such a deeper experience that maybe even had more of an impression than the pains in my life. We really are in this together," Anna says with a peace about her.

Dr. Silver holds up his finger and replies to her, "You are correct, Anna, thank you."

Anna goes on, "Doctor, why are we all here? I don't believe that we were brought here voluntarily. My alarms are going off and something is off about what you told us."

"Anna, you are quite astute." He nods and continues, "It is now that I must reveal the truth to all of you regarding your home worlds. It was too soon before, as you all have other adversities."

"What is it?" Zyus-Pahl worries.

"It is with sadness that I inform you that Planet Earth, Planet Gurrea, and Planet Zor-ah were all destroyed, or now exist without a livable surface."

Anna cries and asks, "What happened, Dr. Silver?"

"Gurrea was destroyed by its star, which went supernova. Zor-ah was hit by a large meteor which wiped out all life. And Earth became a toxic hellscape, destroyed by war and a poisoned environment. Humans disregarded life, so it is now an unlivable place."

"Are we the only ones you saved?" Allegga asks.

"We save as many bright souls from all dying and destroyed worlds as possible," Dr. Silver informs them.

"Oh wow. This is overwhelming," Calvin says as he begins to breathe heavily.

"I know, Calvin," Belle hugs him, and it hits the rest of the travelers, who all embrace each other. Except Brian, who sits back and lets Calvin and Belle comfort Anna.

After a minute of silence, Dr. Silver asks in a gentle way, "Anyone want talk about these major events?" He waits for a minute, but it is still quiet. "No? Then, it is time then to go to the last universe in the Construct, the Mind Over Matter Universe."

"That one, while informative, is not really a creative name, is it?" Calvin smirks at Dr. Silver.

"True. I guess we should really work on some of the names, huh?" Dr. Silver looks at Nurse Goode.

"Maybe." She looks at the doctor, "Has anyone ever complained?"

"Probably, but it's just a name of a universe. If they are straight in the catalog, right?" The doctor turns to his controls, "Okay, glad that is settled. Moving on."

The IAV lifts off the orb and up into orbit away from the magnificent beings, then out of the universe through a small piece of a fragment of a quark...

Chapter 15: Mind Over Matter Universe

In this universe of consideration, with a rendering of the will to make fair all that life can experience, physical laws allow for all living things to have enough. It is a decent expanse, and more than a few galaxies spin and expand throughout this realm.

Extraordinary beings coast through space, all with different compositions from rock to gold to lead, and without any apparent opposition. Their faces differ enough to assume they may have occasional squabbles or perhaps tell jokes when not on a trek.

In a small blip, the IAV emerges and comes to a stop near a cluster of galaxies. A few of the large beings gather, then cruise into one of the spirals. Dr. Silver speaks up, "Here we are, in the last regular universe of our journey, the Mind over Matter Universe. You can see those giants in space, right? Those guys are Elementals, and they can manipulate their elements and use their great size to protect life. We'll follow them into the galaxy."

The craft flies through space and catches up to an elemental giant made of platinum. It looks over at the IAV and smiles.

Zyus-Pahl is confused, "They can see us, Doctor?"

"No, there is one below us. We're in line of sight. These guys are not like the ones in the last universe. That one we are following is a Platinum Elemental."

"They seem like they'd be fun to watch from your home," Calvin says.

"I agree. Think any of the greedy assholes from back home would try melt down the gold one?" Anna jumps in.

Calvin and Belle are the only ones to laugh, and Calvin adds, "They'd all kill each other trying figure out who owned it. Platinum? Sold! Silver and Copper. Are there any species who try to destroy them?"

Dr. Silver replies, "SOO?"

SOO replies, "Yes, and it is a great sin to poach. The great beings intervene between warring species and defend themselves from poachers. Poachers in this universe are so adept at hunting Elementals because they not only gain the wealth by physically dismantling the giant into its raw value, but they also acquire its hyper-brain."

"What is a hyper-brain? I mean, I get that it's bigger than a normal person's." Allegga asks.

SOO answers them, "They have an immortal Hyper-Brain, which connects to the Quantum Dimension to create its element. If the pirates can establish a link with the brain, they can locate other Elementals to dismantle. You would probably ask yourself how a group of life forms could take down one of them, but one way to kill them is by decapitation."

Brian takes the floor, "They decapitate it, and sell off its body. That is what life does. Most planets and most people are destructive, except for a few universes. There is no mystery to any of it. Things belong where they belong. Everyone has people that love them. Except those that don't. But people don't care. People don't care that people are lonely. People are too busy, greedy, and whatever else, life goes on, right? Life goes on, and..."

Calvin stops him, "Funny, I thought you just complained about greedy people and that they don't care. You sound a bit hypocritical there."

"Yeah, you have some nerve, Brian. Who are you to bitch about others? I get that you lost people, but did any of them screw you for you to be so cynical? Why do you antagonize us?"

"I'm not cynical, you're twisting things around. Whatever." He sits back, "You guys are too sensitive and should all calm down. Just calm down." Brian deflects their just criticism. "I'm ready to move on. Do any of these giants make friends with the people here?" Brian asks the doctor.

Calvin is unsettled in his seat. Belle touches his arm as she gives Brian a look, while the Gurrs and Zor-ahns look outside at the wonders.

Dr. Silver looks at Brian and becomes off balance a touch in his reply, "It's always possible, but SOO, do you have any record of a friendship between the giants and life forms?"

SOO smiles and replies, "Yes, a few times. It is not only possible, but it helps when a bond is forged. The life form becomes a valued member of their community, and world." The Orb with limbs continues, "They typically choose individuals who value harmony and compassion."

They travel alongside the giant as it enters a star system, and reach a planet covered in smoke and clouds. The great being stops in the planet's orbit and scans the atmosphere. Dr. Silver keeps the craft alongside it, so they can see if its expressions give anything away. Another giant, made of rock, reaches the world and leads the two into the atmosphere. The IAV follows to see a volcano erupt, blasting a plume of smoke skyward, and the village ahead.

"Whoa, a volcano!" Calvin is excited.

"Those people down there, Dr. Silver!" Belle points to a village's people fleeing the area.

"Just wait one minute," the doctor assures them.

The IAV floats above to observe the ensuing action. The platinum giant lands between the crowd and the volcano and prompts them to climb onto his hands. When the slowest ones climb aboard, the giant walks out and places them in a safe area.

As the other Elemental gets clear with the people, the rock giant slams into the volcano, fists first, and clogs the output. It lets out one more single, tiny poof. As the giant pulls itself out of the volcano, the Rock Elemental punches deep again, then reaches down and shuffles some of the planet guts around.

Zyus-Pahl says, "I love the violence of volcanoes. Such raw, contained pressure, and then it all goes boom!"

Igbogga holds Allegga and says, "I'm terrified of them."

"This inspires me. I'll be back." Belle drops below.

The IAV leaves the planet's atmosphere and cruises back to the surrounding space where more giants roam.

"What is the significance of this universe, Dr. Silver?" Anna asks him.

"Anna, this universe is another example of what a Creator can do with their laws of physics and pyramid of life. These Elementals were once mortal souls who, now immortal, help balance the vulnerable life and the cruelty of space. They can divert most dangers and limit genocides. They can provide a clearer path for this deity or the primary of the world to live among the common souls of a world."

Belle returns and Calvin kisses her.

"Dr. Silver, what else is there in this universe? I think it's cool, but I think I may be ready to move on from here," Calvin says.

"Calvin, we were thinking of going to the moon where the poachers do their work," Dr. Silver then smiles to the group.

Calvin changes his mind, "Okay, sure no problem. Let's go see the poachers dismantle one of the Elementals. I *would* like to see what a hyper-brain looks like, and what type of place can contain such a thing." He looks at Belle, with a smirk, "We change subjects pretty fast around here."

Dr. Silver looks at Nurse Goode, "We're good to go there, right? We have time before The Cradle?"

Nurse Goode nods, "Yes, we can go see that moon. SOO, can you send Dr. Silver the coordinates for the top poacher in the universe?"

SOO flashes their lights, "I can. It is a moon that orbits a gas giant, out of sight and large enough to house the body of an Elemental."

Dr. Silver replies, "Thank you, SOO. Let's take a ride."

The craft takes off from the surface into space, and the travelers are delighted with various Elementals. Once they enter a star system, they can see a gas planet and its many moons.

Dr. Silver points ahead, "It's in that small grouping of moons there." There is a group of eight moons, many of which are rock and ore, and a few are water and ice. Many have artificial lights on the surface. A spacecraft shoots towards an Elemental, whose slow pace and disoriented way prompts Dr. Silver to follow. "Let's see if..."

They cruise to a stop near the Elemental, who becomes startled by the locals' spacecraft. The giant tries to swat the ship, but it slides around the slow mover. The small ship darts up to the giant's neck, and with a razor thin red laser, the Elemental's head is separated from its body.

"That was awful, just awful," Anna is disgusted.

Brian smiles in joy, "What do you mean? That was so cool! Now they're packing it up."

The ship extends arms that package the head and the body and attach small boosters to them. Dr. Silver explains, "Now, they take their treasure back to their moon and get to work on it. SOO, do the Elementals go after the poachers?"

The locals journey back to their moon, booty in tow. The IAV coasts behind, with a good view of the pull. There are no objections from other giants, and the packages arrive at the moon intact.

SOO answers, "I have record of it, but they try to focus on saving innocent lives. If they catch a group trying to do it, and other giants are near, they will exterminate that rogue population."

"The good of the many, right?" Calvin adds.

"Yes, true. Let's follow them inside their base." Dr. Silver flies them with the ship into a huge landing bay that is an open channel through the moon.

Calvin can't believe it, "They cut out this mega hole through the whole moon? What kind of technology does that?"

"SOO?"

SOO answers, "The technology achieved with the help of the hyper-brain allows nearly any possible design or thought to become a reality. Some of the information is so complicated, they have three hypers connected. It is their grouping of the eight moons, all in use by these people. Very advanced."

Anna asks, "Is there a chance we could see one of these brains?"

The doctor nods to Anna, "Yes, let me just..." The craft flies through the large bay to a great cavern with built structure where the late giant's head is held. "Okay, yes. We are in the room where they will extract the brain and send the head back to the body for melt down."

The IAV floats at nose level as the head comes apart to reveal a glowing, light blue brain with a small amount of yellow fluid, and sparks between the uncountable contours.

"Far out, man. That is some space gore there," Brian gets a kick out of the gross sight.

Dr. Silver looks at everyone, a worn-out group, and asks them, "Are there any thoughts or feelings anyone needs to express? I am going to take us out, but slow enough to enjoy the sights while we talk. This will all be gone if they're caught."

The IAV leaves the moon of relentless advancement, and its star system. Just outside, in the galactic neighborhood, a large gathering of

Elementals meet while they stare into the system the travelers just left. The travelers all smile at them, then look ahead as the craft picks up speed.

"You know what I saw? I saw a people, those poachers, who take God's wonderful creations, the Elementals, and shame themselves by destroying these creatures. Nature is different everywhere, but some things should be left alone. We saw this on Earth repeatedly. And here, just as crazy. Especially, when these Elementals are trying to help you," Anna makes a cocktail at her console. Whee-Pahl and the Gurrs do the same.

Brian isn't impressed, "Big deal."

"You know what? Doc? Why are we all on this trip? I mean, really? Or I get why the seven of us were brought on board. We're all decent people, but Brian seems to just make me want to sock him in the face," Calvin says with a hint of humor.

"Even I want to take a swing at him, and I am not a violent Gurr," Igbogga insists.

Dr. Silver puts his hands up to assure the group, "Yes, yes, I know. Brian Harper is a tough cookie and pushes buttons sometimes. However, we take people who are self-aware who trend to optimism and hope. But we also take a person who doesn't completely know good from bad. And, we have another whose mind is in the middle, but his heart is on the correct path. The chaos within the order. Brian, it is always up to you to find your own drive and will. That is what God gives all of us. Losing so many loved ones so close to together is a crushing pain that can break anyone, but you can still learn to thrive again, eventually."

Zyus-Pahl jumps in, "Or you can work through the pain before it gets you."

Calvin raises his hand, "I agree. I have to always push myself in a positive direction or my mind drops into a 'darkness' I find difficult to escape from. My mental illness- "

Dr. Silver stops Calvin, "Sorry, Calvin. Forgive me for cutting you off. I want to let Brian speak if he wants to, because we can't all team up on anyone and expect them to get where we are really coming from. Brian, what do you think?"

"I think it's fun to listen to you all act like you know me or what I'm thinking. I'll figure out what I need to figure out when I feel like I want to figure out what I am going to figure out."

Calvin smirks, "Good one."

Igbogga jumps in, "I would like to say something. I just realized I haven't woken up in the middle of the night since we've been here. My Sexsomnia must be going away, right? Oh, and my cysts are mostly gone! Amazing, Doctor!"

"Yeah, I'm pissing like a racehorse, Doc," Brian says.

"How are you sleeping?" Calvin asks him but gets only a side glance.

Dr. Silver claps his hands, "That's great, Igbogga! And, glad to hear you are feeling better, Brian." He looks at Belle like he forgot she was there, "Belle Cantrell, what do you think?"

"I'm grateful I met Calvin," Belle says as she and Calvin kiss each other. The others, except Brian, smile and enjoy the warmth of the moment. Brian keeps quiet and to himself.

"Very nice. Very, very nice. We are about to travel beyond the 10th Dimension now, so I want you all to open your mind. We will be tested, but I have faith in all of you." The couple stops kissing and they smile at the two hosts. Dr. Silver smiles back and hits his tablet. "Now, let's go to the catalog."

The IAV darts out of an empty space in the corner of a flash...

Chapter 16: The Cradle

No mortal mind could accurately describe this extensive corridor of Existence beyond their own universe, let alone what lie in higher dimensions. Yet, the spirit within connects, when at ease, to learn a few aspects of infinity. There are two Gods in a perpetual motion around the dynamic movements of the relevant Time Space Dimensional Construct within their grasp. From the Construct, and stretching to the ceiling, a visible braid of energies ascends to another part of Existence.

Here, no element up to a molecule in any physical state of matter exists, other than the Construct and its shepherds. It could easily be perceived as the shape of a rectangular box lined with a sort of fiery flesh, but not so simple is the design which houses such an unending complexity inside.

Somewhere between a glow and an inferno of serenity, the realm also features purple electricity in an ever-changing bubble around the cluster of universes and their realities. An occasional IAV travels into the box without measure and rests in a top corner for observation, before it escapes through the roof.

Through a crevice between two passing universes, the IAV shoots up into the expanse between the two great beings. It startles a few of the travelers. Dr. Silver notices and reassures them, "Take some deep breaths. It's okay to be scared, but it's a safe place. I realize the proportion here is quite massive and it can shake your core. We are in what is known as the Cradle. The 11th Dimension. SOO, can you give us some information on the Cradle?"

SOO answers the doctor, "The Time Space Dimensional Construct, our home just below us, rests within this 11th Dimension, or the Cradle. The Cradle is tended to on infinite cycles by these Outer-beings, Oo and Ee, who absorb and redistribute energy, and regulate all consciousness, with the use of Dark Matter and Energy. And so, you'll find the purpose of Dark Matter and Energy, which is that it carries Consciousness and Energy everywhere."

Brian nods his head and says without a strong emotion, "This is far out, I must admit. The scale of these guys, wow. And, finally, I have the answer to Dark Matter and Energy."

Allegga looks at Brian and loses their smile a bit, "So much is hard to believe out here. I am trying to figure it all out."

Igbogga holds Allegga and adds, "It may be best to learn from a place of humility. This is beyond our gigantic universe, and by a great proportion."

Calvin is in awe, and he has no words. He gazes out to the chamber and makes a drink on his console. Belle and a few others join in to quench their thirsts.

Dr. Silver approves of the group energy, but Brian's vibes are low and still. He looks at SOO, "Do you have more information on Oo and Ee?"

The Orb answers, "Yes, they communicate beyond thought, so we won't hear them. Oo and Ee know what we are thinking and doing every moment we are here in their Cradle. The 11th Dimension is part of what is known as the Eternal Pattern of Cradles, or the 12th Dimension. All life and every universe are developed throughout the Eternal Pattern."

Dr. Silver notices a factoid on his tablet and adds, "Humans of a certain religion, Hinduism, know Oo and Ee as Shiva, the God of Consciousness, and Shakti, the Goddess of Energy."

Belle's eyes pop, "Those are the Hindu Gods of Shiva and Shakti? I align with some of the teachings of Hinduism and its peaceful ways."

Calvin doesn't believe it, "You, a girl from the South? Not a criticism, just surprised. It's cool." She smiles at him. He continues once they hold hands, "We're beyond the 10 dimensions now? Existence is so vast. What does the Eternal Pattern look like?" Calvin asks.

"Yes, we're beyond, Calvin. We're going to observe the Eternal Pattern in a moment. Does anyone wish to observe this place anymore? I can wait," Dr. Silver asks them.

No one answers, but a silence takes over as another IAV passes by them and goes through the ceiling of the Cradle.

"How many tours you guys got going?" Zyus-Pahl asks.

"We have many tours. There are many worlds in danger where there are individuals worth saving, so we do just that." The doctor says as a matter of fact, then takes the IAV through a corner of the Cradle.

The craft cruises through the pinkish red boundary, into a thick membrane, of sorts. They come upon a pocket, and there are a few resting IAVs in a small circle. A couple have transformed into houses or huts, but still most remain as their IAV.

Brian speaks up, "Can we visit them? Maybe relax for a moment?"

"Does anyone object to a visit?" Dr. Silver asks the group.

Nurse Goode shakes her head, "Doctor, we must keep moving. These people are in danger here."

"A low-risk danger, Nurse. If they don't disrupt the flow of Existential Energy. Well, maybe it's a higher risk. Who knows why they all stopped though, and I think we should ask someone. Who wants to party with these other travelers to figure out why they stopped? Then, we bug out," Dr. Silver makes the tentative plan. "Just a few of us need to go."

"I'm in," Brian volunteers.

Calvin and Belle raise their hands and she says, "We're in."

Dr. Silver follows, "Okay, the four of us is good. Let's go." The craft enters the pocket and lands near another IAV. Some of the others outside notice the newcomers, with no ill will at the party. The foursome exits the vessel and walks to the crowd.

"It's funny how we breathe everywhere. How is that?" Calvin asks the doctor.

"Because these people created a bubble with the IAV technology." They reach the crowd of different types of people, all mingling and drinking various fancy drinks and waters.

"Hello, I am Quan Silver, and these three fine individuals travel with me and my wife. May we join you all?" Calvin and Belle share a smile after he says his first name.

A tall woman speaks up, "Yes of course, you can join us. I am Emeva Drokwilth, and we are just gathering here before continuing with our journey."

"Are you an Operator, like me?"

"I am. One of my passengers suggested we create our own bubble here, beyond time and space, and just chill out. Someone from a place called Earth."

"You don't say. We have a few of them as well. I would like you to meet Brian, Belle, and Calvin. We just wanted to see if there was an issue with your travels."

As he says that, the place starts to shake a bit. Then, it rumbles to shake the IAVs. Dr. Silver turns around, "Let's go now!" The little party breaks up. He and his Human guests dart back to their craft and rejoin their party without a word.

They take off with some of the other vessels, and just in time they look behind to see the pocket collapse! It crushes the last couple of crafts as they were transforming back from huts. The IAV shoots up to through the membrane, and the doctor continues, "We just must travel through the considerable distance of the membrane. Ah, here we go."

Anna shakes her head, "I'm glad we stopped."

Zyus-Pahl and Whee-Pahl shake their heads.

The craft exits the membrane, in haste, and rests along the edge of a nauseating pattern of infinity— spanning and waving into geometric confusion towards a black abyss.

"Wow, I think I want to puke," Belle hides her eyes, then looks again. "I'm good with the 12th dimension, I think."

"Yeah, I'm good too, Doc," Calvin holds Belle's hand.

"Okay already?" He looks at a bunch of dizzy folks. "Okay, good enough." Dr. Silver turns the vessel around and punches back through the membrane. They continue nonstop to return to the same top corner and the view of the great Gods, Oo and Ee.

"What is the difference between life in each Cradle and life in each universe along 10 dimensions? I mean, are there infinite versions of each of us?" Brian asks.

Dr. Silver answers, "SOO?"

SOO replies, "Each Cradle holds a different version of every single universe along its 10 dimensions, so each of our souls exist in every way within that. However, all Cradles hold different Constructs with different universes and different souls to preserve variance and balance."

"Still confused but it's okay." Belle thinks for a second, "Maybe it's not actually that complex. I just realized I sometimes cut off a thought when I don't feel like thinking about it. It causes me to not think for myself sometimes, and it makes me doubt my skills and intelligence."

Anna looks at Belle, "You seem plenty smart to me, Belle."

"And I noticed you are also plenty confident, Belle, as well," Dr. Silver smiles at her.

"Thank you, kindly." She looks at everyone and continues, "What we are doing is so crazy and nothing like anything I've experienced. It is really making me think. Do you know what I mean, Cal?"

"Definitely. After many cycles of mania and depression, anxiety and worry, then periods of happiness and balance, I learned my strengths and tendencies that were bringing me relief and the thinking that contributed to my suffering. Facing the pain and processing it, and not getting angry, but staying cool. I used to lose my calm and end up entertaining the simple minded."

"Well said, both of you. I mean, you both are considerable thinkers. We will continue to journey through this realm and straight to the next one where everything known is seen and learned for the One God. First, we must learn about Oo and Ee. Unlike you and me, Oo and Ee are the same in every Cradle. So named for the divine sounds of Harmony and Chaos. Any questions?" Before the doctor there is a quiet group still staring outside.

Nurse Goode taps the doctor on the shoulder, "Doctor, were we going to show the nature of the universes too?"

"Oh, yes, thank you Nurse. Let's take a trip up to the center of the realm." He drives the IAV from the corner to the center of the realm, directly above the two gargantuan Gods. Between them, they go into the light streaming to the Cradle's ceiling.

As the craft stops, Dr. Silver points the nose downward to view the top of the dynamic cluster of universes. They see particles pass by them; bright little dots that effervesce faint, sparse suds, and go through the ceiling of the Cradle. Up close, they feel the channel of blue and yellow lights as a touch of bliss takes over.

"SOO, can you please tell us what is going on here?" Dr. Silver waves to the robot and the lights passing through."

SOO stands up, gathers a few little dots with its metal hand, and spreads the lights across the air ahead, "This is love and positivity, simple as that. But this is pure love, from the experiences of all life in all universes. When you are in the moment, and you cannot see it, but lovers create this. I am an Omnipresent quantum computer, so I can tell you that Calvin and Belle created a few pieces of this. So have Zyus-Pahl and Whee-Pahl. And so have Allegga Goleeka and Igbogga Goleeka, along with the doctor and nurse. Wonderful group, Dr. Silver. Maybe yours are all indistinguishable from the others, but they're here."

Calvin kisses Belle and they make out for a moment. The other two couples kiss, so Anna drops below, which leaves Brian alone to watch them all make out. Within a second or two, little dots of light come out of all the partners.

SOO watches in delight as a flow of light shines from the four couples, then Dr. Silver interjects, "How about we all take a break now before we go to the next thrilling leg of the journey?" The couples descend to the lower level, then the doctor turns to Nurse Goode, "Would you like to go climb all over each other for a little while?"

Dots of light go through Brian as he drops to his cabin last with a bit of indifference. The IAV floats in the center of the Cradle emitting solid blue and yellow dots of light, which pour up through the ceiling.

Calvin lifts slowly, a steaming cup of coffee in hand, to an empty IAV. He sips a couple times as the lights of love stream through the craft. Belle joins him and smiles, "They're not here, huh?" Calvin shakes his head, and she joins him in his seat. "This is all so..."

"I know. What is all this? I'm grateful I'm not alone in this unbelievable experience and knowledge. Right?" Calvin is out of his gourd.

"Yeah, and there's more."

Dr. Silver and Nurse Goode return, as do the others one at a time, to the canopy part of the vessel. Quiet greetings pass between them as they arrive. The doctor grabs his tablet and looks around his station, "Ah yes." The doctor turns to them and goes on, "Now, we're going to the next place in our exploration, the Quantum Reflection. We will travel straight through the beam of lights and into the core of the universes."

"Yeah, I'm tired of the of all the love in the Cradle," Brian exercises his dark empathic abilities with a slow exhale, and the cabin goes quiet. There is no energy between any of them. He continues, "So, where is it? The Quantum Reflection?" Brian asks.

"Um, yes, Brian. I will only be able to describe the place when we get there, too."

"Something is different. What's going on?" Calvin looks around at the others and finishes his thought, "I don't feel so good." Belle grabs his hand, but with his other hand, Calvin rubs his eyes in distress.

"Yes, there is indeed," Dr. Silver nods. "Ready to go? Maybe we should move on."

"Sounds good to me. What do you think?" Belle nudges Calvin, who holds her tight. The rest of the group remains silent. A few grab a drink.

"Yes, hold on," Dr. Silver says as he turns the IAV down into the beam of light and shoots into it. He hits a button and the canopy darkens a few shades. They fly by the swirling and massaging appendages of the Outer-beings, and into the cluster of universes.

Space and time seem to alter as they pass by the other realms, unaware of the lifeforms observing them. The IAV speeds up and shoots as it shrinks until they see huge building blocks of energy and matter, which then get smaller. A rhombus shape, shining many colors, draws them inside through its flat face, like a drop of water...

Chapter 17: The Infinite Collection and The Quantum Reflection

Understanding it all, when all is available to be understood, includes the all-knowing Quantum dimension, one half the size of God. It reflects all physical dimensions, or the balancing side of Existence where predestination and coincidence are common occurrences. And, it is cherished with an unconditional love, as endowed to life.

Oh, Great Lord, thou hath begun Existence with this Infinite count of immortal life forms, the Collection, to oversee all mortal life. Creators and Primary Spirits, the eternal and the exalted, are brought upon to encourage and preserve life in respect to this Collection: the origin of consciousness in all worlds and realms.

All tangible and intangible concepts of life and time are regulated within the portent of this portion of Existence. This ever dynamic range from inert to wild to controlled assemble to mirror all physical infinities and eternities within the Eternal Pattern of Cradles. Beings of a neutral color manage it all, both seen and unseen at the same time, in a place with deep purple hues and webs of lightning that fill the outlines of a minority of worlds.

In a piece of foggy haze, a rhombus appears and the IAV emerges from it on a slow coast. The concept behind them disappears and reappears nearby, but without another interference. The craft floats in this disorienting place, then extends glowing purple arms from the base.

As the purple arms reach out, they spark electricity or something like it. "What is that purple stuff out there we are making with the

IAV?" Calvin asks.

Dr. Silver answers him, "Dark Matter and Energy originate here in the Quantum Reflection. That is our Dark Matter flight module and the electricity it emits is Dark Energy."

"Why do we need Dark Matter and Energy to travel?" Allegga asks.

Dr. Silver answers him, "Our travels allow us to go in all dimensions and sometimes require different methods. This is the only part of the journey we have this. In all others, the Near Instant travel happens by skipping the physical element of those dimensions. These arms use consciousness and energy, like Oo and Ee. Is that a good explanation? Sometimes I just talk."

"It makes as much sense as a lot of this that just goes over my head, but it sounds right," Zyus-Pahl admits.

Brian follows, "I get it."

"I think I get it, but it is all still too mammoth to think about. So, where are we?"

"We are in the Quantum Dimension! Ahead, out there, you may... Oh wait." He hits a button on the dash, and the canopy lightens up to reveal the nauseating size of the dimension and the many, many Cradles and Constructs. "The Quantum Dimension is the Reflection of all Known and Future Existences. It is managed by beings that are immortal and each pair up with a livable spirit, which helps make the Reflection. SOO, do you have any information on these beings?"

They look out and see some of the beings within Constructs, inside universes, and on worlds. They behave without aggression and communicate without words. They have thin but smooth bodies with gray skin, and large heads with great, black eyes.

SOO smiles and points to the beings, "They are of a familiar face and form, but usually mistaken for mortal beings of another world. They are the Greys, also known as The Collection, all immortal and infinite. The origin of many nightmares of abductions and implants and influencing evolution on many planets. However, Greys are the origin and subconscious of all souls, including Primary Souls, Creators, and all life forms. They know all that occurs within the 12 dimensions, their charge, but do not reflect Oo and Ee. Their infinite number reflects the infinite number of Cradles and the Constructs of universes they house. Infinity is infinity, after all."

"And, so together, they make up The Infinite Collection and The

Quantum Reflection, or the 13th Dimension. Watch the Greys long enough and you'll find patterns and familiar movements that are like a picture that captures light in the opposite way," Dr. Silver tells them.

"You mean a negative to a photograph?" Belle says it is obvious.

"Yes, I suppose, but different people say different words occasionally. Thank you, I didn't have a name for it. SOO, any other facts or trivia we can learn right now?"

"Do you all want to see your Grey selves, or your 'mirror', now or later?" SOO asks the doctor.

"I'm not sure that I want to see that, but maybe," Calvin says in complete disbelief.

"I'll meet mine," Belle says with confidence.

Allegga speaks their mind, "Sounds like fun to me." Igbogga isn't sure but stays in their partner's arms.

Brian is last, but in a monotone voice, "I'm in."

"SOO, I think they do. It is the spiritual healing of origin and depth that a connection can offer. Did you ever wonder why being in love is so beautiful? That is when you and another life form share that bond of love, and your Greys reflect a harmonizing warmth that carries through Existence."

"That is so cool," Anna says and earns a few nods. Brian is still and stoic.

Dr. Silver responds to her, "I agree, Anna." He turns around and the IAV takes off by the push of the deep purple energy.

SOO looks at the couple and continues, "You must be prepared, for they are you in every way except they project your inside back to you. They are *not* evil, my friends. They are that they are."

"We are on our way and know that travel here is not by distance but by awareness. We have a lock. Alright, let's prepare ourselves. Listen to me right now when I say to stay positive in yourself," The doctor is stern in his instructions.

"That is sometimes extremely difficult for me, Dr. Silver. My mental illness is half negative. What will my Grey be like?" Calvin is uneasy yet curious.

"You'll have to wait and see. We can only guess, but the Doctor and I have done a few hundred tours, and few good folks like yourself have had bad results here. Just stay positive. They're almost like angels, but it can go awry," Nurse Goode shares with them.

"Yes, this is all deeply personal, and the Grey will not look like you, which you should know as well. But you will be connected in essence."

Igbogga shakes a bit and pulls away from Allegga to get a drink. Whee-Pahl initiates an embrace with her husband. Brian sips his water and watches all of them act naturally.

Calvin fidgets with his spin-fidgeter. He spins it for a few seconds, then stops it and puts it back in his pocket. "I think I'm getting some anxiety about this," Calvin's heart rate increases.

Dr. Silver sees a readout on his tablet and tells them, "Take a few breaths, we are a minute away... in our measure of time."

The passengers remain quiet while watching the uncountable worlds and the Greys go about their chaotic and ordered behaviors with some grace.

The IAV goes through the haze of the unknown. The travelers see the shadows of life's chaos, as shown by the Greys, to reveal the true points of view of immortals, without causing any type of destruction.

"Is that another IAV approaching?" Calvin asks, then it hits him, "It's us."

"It is us," Dr. Silver smiles as the other IAV pulls up to them.

The two crafts turn broadside to face each other. There are ten Greys who mime the people, in perfection. The driver is calm but is in proximity with another. Three pairs, behind those two, hold hands and two others sit alone. In one pair, an individual rubs their gut once and the other holds its agonizing head. One other one is still and doesn't make much eye contact with anyone, then it looks up with sadness.

Brian makes eye contact with it, and it looks away. He sees Calvin struggle while watching his Grey and says in a false gentle voice, "Don't fall apart, boy."

Calvin looks at Brian, and responds, "Get the hell out of here. You were right, Dr. Silver. This is a lot to handle. What do I do from here?" Calvin is off center.

"I'm here, Calvin," Belle grabs his arm, and just as their mirror Greys reflect the same, his Grey stops displaying the raw agony and looks up at Calvin.

Calvin says, "I feel like the pain, deep down, I can see it. I can see how there are twists and past restraints that echo in my mind, keep me spinning around. The pain." Calvin sobs with such fierce wail that feels like cleansing. He slows to a steady tearing and the pain in his eyes makes him grab them. "I'm in such pain right now. Belle, I'm sorry you have to see this."

Whee-Pahl tears up and gets scared. As Zyus-Pahl tries to keep her calm, she and her mirror hold their heads and panic. Igbogga looks at their mirror, a submissive pleader, and pushes them into a depression.

The Greys reflect them with their growing number of fallers. Calvin stops the outflow of tears and calms to silence as he sits back up in his seat. Whee-Pahl stops hunching over, and Igbogga tries to put on a tough face, though neither can remain at strength.

"Are you three, okay?" Nurse Goode asks him.

Calvin sits still and looks at Belle and the others, "I'm in such pain, I just want to get away so bad." He grabs his head and struggles, and the mirror flips out inside while holding its head.

Dr. Silver opens his eyes wide, "Calvin, you must not give into the despair while you are here. As all three of you, including your mirrors, fall into a depression, we could lose you."

Belle panics as Calvin now sits catatonic, staring up. "What is that, Dr. Silver?" She asks the doctor. Igbogga and Whee-Pahl also become frozen, in a way.

The two IAVs float next to each other without a hint that they plan to move. Plenty of commotion outside the crafts continues, while inside, they deal with the off-balanced. Through the transparent canopies, one set mimics the other, which seems like a stalemate is at hand.

But, beyond their meet up, a large, black sphere approaches. A couple of them become startled, and Brian simmers a tiny smirk.

Dr. Silver turns to see it approach them and announces to them, "It's the Great Void. It can take you from us. You have found your own source of love, both inward to yourself and outward to all— if you want to escape!"

Igbogga shakes their head and whimpers, which repulses Allegga a bit, so Igbogga hangs their head in shame. Whee-Pahl holds her face and while Zyus-Pahl attempts to help her, she resists him.

The Great Void, a perfect black sphere, comes to a rest next to the two crafts, and pulls out Calvin, Whee-Pahl, and Igbogga from their IAV. Brian goes last, then the Darkness vanishes without warning.

"Oh my God!" Belle looks at Dr. Silver and Nurse Goode, "Can we get them?!"

Dr. Silver is unsure in his reply, "Yes, but we need them to overcome what holds them down. We made this whole journey and usually folks have a handle on things. I thought we were all good here, except for maybe Brian, who went to the Great Void with Aurfuud. I see he couldn't overcome his challenge."

"Let's go!" Belle is a frantic mess. Zyus-Pahl and Allegga are with her.

"Yes, definitely, Belle," Dr. Silver turns and hits his controls as the mirror craft does the same, and they simultaneously turn away from each other.

The IAV cruises through the haze and the remaining six keep quiet.

"We're approaching, Doctor," Nurse Goode says as the rhombus comes into view.

"Thank you, Nurse. We're not going through the rhombus this time, but between it. Pay attention so you can tell the others about it."

The IAV approaches the rhombus and retracts the Dark Matter flight module. It pierces the parallelogram's surface, only to turn in the middle of the entry, and into the corner...

Chapter 18: The Origin of All

Inside this All-Being of Blessed Divinity, Infinity and Zero are opposite forces in the consideration for all that is conceivable, with degrees of difference and congruency in between all harmony. Negative numbers could align with the concepts of the Collection and the Reflection, but when counting them as part of all of Existence, the two forces house all that exist.

Abstract ideas obstruct the clarity of how pure it is all together. That nothing in its creation can cause it harm. It is that it is. The only words to summarize any feelings here are unconditional love and open truth.

As we pray to the One, we connect and give thanks to the fullness of our life of experiences. Or we can instead meditate, with humility and gratitude, into the vibrations that penetrate every dimension within The One. In either connection, life forms send love and gratitude, flavored by the style of everyone's personality.

Through the rhombus' flat corner, the IAV emerges. It is surrounded by a white glow. They are now beyond the view of the rhombus, beyond the view of only the Quantum Dimension, and beyond the Pattern of Cradles with all their clusters of dimensions. They can see all of everything at once, as they look everywhere.

Allegga and Zyus-Pahl bow their heads, which prompts Belle and Anna to look at each other. They all remain quiet, however, as the craft floats up to a greater view of the One, as Thou chooses to be seen. Both at a distance, and from within, they see now that the concepts of God will always humble a mortal. Let alone, being blessed with this Divine journey.

It is of a familiar design to Belle, who gazes at the greatest wonder, "On my world, they call this a Yin-yang, but God is not the flat picture."

"Like a living one. Something beyond description," Anna is in awe.

"We have heard of that word, Belle," Nurse Goode smiles at her and holds her hand.

"Is this God?" Allegga asks the doctor.

"Yes, Allegga," Dr. Silver confirms her question.

"Where are Calvin and the others?" Belle looks at the Everything before her and around them all.

Dr. Silver looks at SOO, "SOO, can you tell us where Calvin, Igbogga, Whee-Pahl, and Brian are right now? We had to come here first to get there."

SOO answers him, "Yes, Doctor. The Great Void holds Calvin Wayne, Igbogga Goleeka, Whee-Pahl, and Brian Harper. They each struggle to regain their own positive self-images. If we can get them, it is because we can reach them from the All Light, which can bring us to our loved ones across Existence. It is beyond the physical plane, so be prepared to see concepts flash by in moments."

"Thanks, SOO. Let's go!" They shoot across the whole of the Quantum Reflection, so massive it is, and approach the All Light, the sphere of light and love. As the IAV breaks the boundary, everything begins to glow with a keen brightness. They slow to crawl, then stop in place. "Okay, we can get out of here."

"Get out? Get out?!" Belle can't believe him.

"Yes, we can all live in the All Light forever, since nothing ages here. But we are not staying here," Dr. Silver says to them.

Allegga grows impatient, "Can we go get them?"

The doctor turns to Allegga and replies, "Yes, right now, but they have to find their way to the surface of the Great Void."

They all exit the side of the craft and follow the doctor a short distance. It is white everywhere and all around. Belle notices her feet land where she wants them to land. She says to the others, "This is really something— walking here."

Zyus-Pahl responds, "It feels so... I don't know, it is free and easy here. I hope we can get them back."

Dr. Silver continues, "Now, the bad news for Brian is that we can't call him because he has no intimate relationship here with any of us.

Now, I want Belle, Allegga, and Zyus-Pahl to stand towards the open All Light and concentrate on your loved one."

It is a plague of despair and aftermath all around, as the Great Void is where all fears, regrets, and terrors are fulfilled and brought to the dimensions of life and love. Darkness is all around. Hints of others, who whisper their projections onto whomever dares listen, make this the origin of nightmares.

Aurfuud's echoing faces watch over Brian as the human realizes his powers in the dark place. He projects a knoll in a grass field, then a snowy park, then he flies up and around. The demon has seen enough, "Be still."

Brian Harper stops the projections, then stands still in the emptiness. Without emotion while looking around, he asks, "Is that you, Darkness?" Aurfuud's many faces smile and it disappears.

The large beast, with its glowing eyes, slips out of the fog and smoke, then circles him. It speaks, "I'm glad you are not alone."

Brian clears his throat and replies, "I brought three others with me."

The beast smiles, "That will do, for now. But we don't have them for good yet, so we'll pull them down further."

As they dash away, each of them leaves a trail of smoky shadows. Brian suggests, "Whee-Pahl is the smallest and most vulnerable one to recruit. Let's get her first."

After a moment, they arrive at a depressed and worried Whee-Pahl, who fails to lift her head.

In the Darkness, Brian and the Wolf bring along with them the timid Whee-Pahl. Poor Whee-Pahl, so scared and wondering how she got there. Everything smells too.

They quickly arrive near Igbogga Goleeka, whose head hangs low. Their chin touches their chest while they rest on a log. It rains a slow drip that pierces instead of soothes. They scratch their head in shame, lost in a thought. Even if it is *just* a thought.

Brian sneaks up behind them while the Wolf stands behind him, still, and holds Whee-Pahl. He whispers in their ear, "You should feel less than Allegga. They are the strong one. You wish you were strong like them, that's why you feel so weak and ashamed."

Igbogga cries and rubs their head, then yells out, "No! No way! That is not true!"

Brian smiles as he sits next to Igbogga on the log, "Now, Igbogga, I have Whee-Pahl over there." Before he points, the Wolf turns into a large tree, next to the female Zor-ahn. "See? Whee-Pahl is on board, and you know you can trust her. That doctor was only after one thing, and that was to bring more people to a fantasy land. Here, I can live however I want to live, and with whatever I want. Help me, and we can live forever here."

Igbogga looks at Brian, then the tree turns back to the Wolf. They say, "Where is Calvin? Is he here? I saw him when we were taken. Just him. Now, you two are here asking me to stay in this scary dark place forever. I want Allegga and I want them now."

In between Igbogga and Whee-Pahl, a bright white spot appears. The Wolf gets fueled and runs in between the light and the Gurr. Igbogga jumps, and while looking around at Brian and a sad Whee-Pahl, the light disappears.

Brian smiles, "Igbogga, let me show you and Whee-Pahl a place where you can feel how you want to feel, bad or good." He projects a beautiful beach where Allegga, Zyus-Pahl, and the others from their travels lay out in the sunshine.

Whee-Pahl is confused but still steps through the threshold into the lovely setting, while Igbogga hesitates to take a stand. Igbogga gets up and looks around, then to Brian, "I don't believe you that that is the others. Calvin is here too. I just know it."

"Okay, let's go get Calvin. I know he is in a dark place, so you may be in danger," Brian says as he sees Whee-Pahl content in her illusion. "Don't say a word to Calvin, unless I say it's okay."

Calvin lies down on his back in a black puddle, ensconced in dread. He lifts his head, then sits up. The Human looks everywhere he can look, then hangs his head in sadness.

What was that sound? I swear I heard something. It was so dark and... What happened to the others. Am I, what is... I feel so sad, please don't let me fall here again.

A black cloud pours over Calvin like dense smoke. As it disappears, his face has the dusty remnants of it. He wipes his face and lays back, but as the black puddle tries to swallow him, he jumps up and avoids the nightmare. Calvin stands up and cleans himself off, then looks around.

While Calvin mixes inside himself, it allows Brian, the Wolf, and Igbogga to arrive without a sound. Brian puts on his face of fake sympathy, and says, "Hey, Calvin, I know you and I haven't always gotten along, but I can help you here. You don't have to worry about your mental problems here. I even brought Igbogga along, who said they wanted to see you because they knew you were here too." Brian points to Igbogga, who walks up to them from behind the Wolf.

Igbogga doesn't smile when they speak, "Hi Calvin. I trust you. What should we do?"

Brian jumps in, "I can give you a peaceful place where you don't have to think about your emotions or problems. Just enjoy the things that are enjoyable."

Calvin struggles, "Yeah, I just... I feel hazy, like I can't think straight. I'm so sick of feeling so down all the time. It's so painful to live like that all the time."

Brian smiles a bit, "You don't have to feel that anymore. Here, you can be with Belle forever in this perfect setting." He projects a place before Calvin that is a farmhouse, with a large yard, where Belle and some friends enjoy a barbecue. Before Igbogga, he projects a fancy room, decorated in flowing silk and chandeliers, with tables of indulgent food and drink. The two begin to walk into the illusions.

I... I must change something; there is something off and I can't figure it out. I love her. Her. Belle? No, this is not Belle. Something else is pulling me in here, but I need to get back to Belle. This place feels so easy though. I could eat some ribs...

The Wolf nods at Brian as the two prisoners begin to seal themselves into the Darkness. Brian produces a lounge chair with a drink on an end table. He sits and sips.

No, this isn't right. I know this isn't right. Belle feels different than this. I love the potential of my life and what I've overcome so far. I am so lucky and I feel like this place... It isn't right for me. I'm getting out of here. I love myself and I love my Belle...

Calvin exits his illusion, to the disdain of Brian and the Darkness, and starts to yell, "Belle! Belle!" He feels his heart hurt, then remembers, "Igbogga!" He tries to run to the other traveler but is slowed down by something. His legs move slowly and he gets fatigued. Calvin thinks for a moment, then begins to float. He feels the light inside of him overpower the Darkness. "Igbogga! We have to leave!"

Igbogga is startled in their fancy feast, "What is this? Allegga?" They jump up and the illusion falls away from them. Oh, my! Oh, we must get Whee-Pahl!"

Calvin grabs the Gurr and they fly through the Darkness, "Concentrate on your friendship with Whee-Pahl and we'll go straight to her." They leave Brian and the Wolf behind, for a minute. They fly past many scenes of folks enjoying a dream life, then arrive at the beach scene where the Zor-ahn female lays out to tan.

Igbogga states, "There she is!"

They swoop down, and pull her out of the dream, which dissipates instantly. She is startled, "What was... Hey, you took me from Zyus and our relaxing vacation."

Calvin replies, "Whee-Pahl, it's me Calvin and Igbogga. We have to leave. I think we have to think about our loved ones on the IAV, but I'm not sure. It seems like the right thing to do." They stop in a dark place together, holding hands to stay firm and positive.

"Stay positive and concentrate?" Igbogga checks with Calvin.

"Yes, just think hard about them."

They remain still and silent, then Brian and the Wolf arrive, "Don't anyone go anywhere."

The trio holds together with a space in between them, and a bright spot appears. It grows and they disappear inside it, leaving Brian behind. He looks at the Wolf, "We lost them!"

"Yes, you failed to keep them here, Brian. We'll keep you, though."

"There they are, Dr. Silver! They're together!" Belle's excitement is relief as well.

"I see them. When they begin to reach through, grab them," Dr. Silver says as they stand in the All Light, waiting.

Darkness creeps into the All Light, and the trio squeezes out, one at a time. They appear together, like they were in the Darkness. "Excellent! I see we are now without Brian, right?"

"Yes, he was the one who tried to keep us there," Igbogga declares. "Thank you for helping to save us, Calvin."

Whee-Pahl agrees, "Yes, once again, Calvin saved me. Thank you, my friend."

Zyus-Pahl echoes her, "Yes, yes, thank you, Calvin."

The group gets back into the IAV, once again at ease. As they all get in and get comfortable, Belle quickly grabs her man for a momentary make out session.

"Of course, let's all celebrate! Then, we'll finish the tour. Cool?" The doctor says to his wife.

"No problem. What were your experiences like in the Great Void?" Nurse Goode asks them.

Whee-Pahl speaks up, "I was scared and confused. Lost, and then on a beach with Zyus. I was in this trance, then I heard Calvin yell for me." She and her man hold each other.

Igbogga follows her, "I was so confused and felt awful about myself, then when Calvin called for me, I realized how I was greater and more loving with my Allegga than the illusion. They played on my darkest thoughts."

"It was complete solitude and sorrow. It felt like I was there a long time before I began to realize I was still alive and had thoughts and feelings. Then, Brian appeared with Igbogga. I was caught in the trap for a moment, but I had the fresh experiences with Belle that brought me home," Calvin gives his account.

Zyus-Pahl says with feeling, "I want to go to my cabin with Whee."

"Of course, we can all take a break right now." As the IAV hovers in the All Light, they all drop below to their cabins.

Their return to the canopy is staggered, where Dr. Silver and Nurse Goode relax with Anna and drinks. Outside, they can see the All Light around. It is silent, but there is a love song playing from 1980's Earth in the IAV.

Dr. Silver turns to his console and says, "We'll now head to the wider view of the One, and I'll continue the tour."

As Calvin returns, he watches them leave the All Light and zoom into a view of the greatness everywhere. He attempts to put it into words, "It's a great yin-yang. Like a three dimensional one that always moves and changes."

Dr. Silver responds, "Well, three dimensional in the concept that we are watching everything, but as Belle guessed, this *is* God. So, with the blessing of being allowed in Thou's presence, I want to tell that this is your Evergrasp. Or your concept of all of Existence."

"My Evergrasp is in need of full reflection," Calvin insists.

"Mine too," Belle smiles with him.

"SOO, do you have any knowledge, so we don't spread a lie in this sacred place?"

SOO explains, "Yes, this is the 14th and Mother Dimension, known by many as God or The One. Thou are beyond any life form or other thing of relevance, from the Pattern and it's inconceivable infinity with the emptiness of the Quantum Dimension. Each contains the other side's essence, the Great Void and the All Light, which in turn creates the livable existence. Only the blessed may travel here to witness Thou. Know that Love and Truth stand above all, and the first thought that divided God so that God could create Existence and life, is that God is the Self Known but split to also become the Self Unknown."

"Thank you, SOO. That was the most important piece of any knowledge on our trip. Just wonderful," Dr. Silver wipes a tear from his eye.

"Wow, thank you for choosing me for this, Dr. Silver." Calvin looks outside the craft.

"I know, Cal, right? I guess my life has been decent since my surgery. I've still had issues, but I've learned lots. This has all totally changed me," Belle says with enthusiasm.

"You are all welcome. Calvin, you conquered your demons on your own. Belle, you've endured physical illness with the belief you will stay that way. Anna, you are whole again. You have all grown, and it is not yet over," Dr. Silver tells them.

"Yes, that last universe?" Allegga asks him.

"We are about to go to your new universe, which is far and away so fantastic, that you will meet beings you thought were made up," Dr. Silver sips some of his drink. "SOO, do you have any more information or knowledge for these special people?"

SOO smiles and answers, "I have some small tidbits. There is a certain flow of the hierarchy of life. The basic life is the amoeba, up to the microbes, to everything from insects to plant networks to animals and people, then up to Primary Souls and Celestials, to their Universal Deity. Last, it is vital to know that praying to send love to God and those around you, spreads Hope to all life. All life."

As they contemplate the knowledge of it all, there are only smiles and lightness. Dr. Silver hits some buttons on SOO, and a tray comes up with seafood, from shrimp to scallops to lobster, to a few mystery items. It rests on top of SOO, who is somewhat dissatisfied being a waiter.

"Is this all-Earth seafood?" Calvin asks. "Oh, what is that?"

"That is Beegar, a delicacy from Gurrea, right?"

Igbogga replies, "Yes, it is. Very tasty."

"Earth seafood, and these other things from Gurrea and Zor-ah, because each is a delicacy to the Ellagantce. We know you all like these things from your menu preferences on our travels. Here are some plates." Dr. Silver grabs the plates from a drawer next to him and passes them to the others. "Who wants to say a prayer?"

Zyus-Pahl raises his hand and the doctor motions back to him, "Dear God, thank you for blessing us with this journey, and please bless this food as we enjoy the company of each other and your Grace."

Belle grabs a couple of shrimp and scallops. Calvin does the same. The others dig in, and no one forgets the sauces and dips. They all make drinks and sit back...

As Dr. Silver puts away the tray, they all look outside again and gaze. SOO smiles and breaks the silence, "We all done eating? Do you still need me as a table anymore?"

"No, thank you, SOO," Dr. Silver says. "Right guys?"

"Yes, thank you, SOO," Calvin says with a smile.

Dr. Silver tells them, "Let's move on. First, though, I want you to all focus on God, be grateful, and say a prayer for all life or anything good."

They all take a moment to themselves and pray. One by one, they finish. Dr. Silver nods with them as they go to the center of the Divine, where the rhombus awaits. They shoot through a microscopic corner of the flat rhombus, inside their home Cradle. Through the corner, they turn and twist up through the top to flash back into the 10th dimension. A few universes go by, then they enter a bright blue one through a small spark...

Chapter 19: We Are Together

With an unrivaled beauty and serenity, this realm of peace has relatively few planets and stars. All around, there is a curious element which elevates all to a state beyond the normal struggles of mortal life forms. Only an open heart can capture the view of this paradise, by trial and ascension.

There are a few, full and billowy, clouds above a blue ombre sky which cast down harmony on mountains and hills and streams and gills, on every world. On one world, specifically, there is a cathedral with a portal to something fantastic beyond it. Lands retain mists to keep comfortable with the ideal combination of a moderate temperature, slight moisture, and a hint of a breeze.

Elegant people of various species wear robes and walk at their own pace among the easy pour of the surrounding waterfalls. Most cathedrals here have a black pool, centered and without a roof, but one has an extraordinary glow and a concave prism of crystal for the roof.

A few of the beautiful beings fly around from planet to planet, with no propulsion or hassle. Just an ease of travel, to this place where all of the beings seem to gather.

Through a small spark inside a fluffy cloud, the IAV shoots into the new universe with a trail of ice behind it. They float out of the cloud and see the small expanse without much deep space.

Dr. Silver turns to the group with a smile, "I would like to welcome you all to the most coveted universe, Heaven." The canopy retracts to give them all fresh air. "This place is different than every other one in the entire 10th dimension. First thing, you may all feel healthy if you didn't before. There is an element in this universe that heals everything. No diseases or illnesses exist here."

"I'm healed here. Wow. I mean, I don't feel off in any way, just tranquil," Calvin smiles at Belle. "Things happen the way they're meant to happen. I am psyched now that I feel whole. And, in love." He turns to Belle.

"It feels good to have that relief, I know," Belle kisses Calvin, then they hug.

Zyus-Pahl feels something, "My back just cracked in a weird way. I feel so able. At last, I can sneeze full volume and clear out the village!"

Whee-Pahl smiles and touches his back, then starts spinning her hands, "My wrists are cooling down. It feels so good! I have my strength back!"

Anna shakes her head side to side, "I think I feel better just from going through everything, but what do I know?" She throws up a fist, provoking a few smirks from the others, then looks down, "Oh, my legs cleared up!"

"Excellent, everyone. I am so happy you all feel well." Dr. Silver asks it, "SOO, can you please tell us a bit about this universe and world here?"

The craft glides along a path around the landscape to a gathering of people walking along stone paths and bridges over small creeks and larger streams. At the gathering, there are white canvas yurts around tables, with a bountiful choice of fare, all spread about. Flowers are everywhere you can decorate them.

SOO explains, "Yes, Dr. Silver. There are no servants here. Some servants ascend to Heaven because they suffer at the expense of a spoiled soul. Eating here is for enjoyment only, and all food is created by will. Just as the weather remains constant and clothes stay clean, wishes never would get wished because maybe they are no longer needed. There are no nights, and no need to sleep, but rest is enjoyed while a cherished soul sends love to God."

"That's beautiful, SOO," Belle wipes a tear. Calvin holds her hand and they kiss again.

"I've seen a few people flying here. Can we fly, Doc?" Calvin asks him.

"Yes, you can do all sorts of things that would have been considered paranormal on your home world," Dr. Silver replies. "I want to congratulate all of you in ascending to the Heaven Universe, where you will be able to do great things. Brian was the wild card, and we had to let him decide if he was a dark soul, or one who could open to God's truths."

The IAV lands on a small piece of grass, with landing gear deployed, and people begin to gather around. The folks begin to chatter and smile, and there are no mocking faces around.

As the door to the IAV opens, Calvin helps Belle out first, then himself. Anna, Igbogga, and Allegga follow, then Zyus-Pahl helps Whee-Pahl out of the tall craft as they both hop down.

Applause and cheers from all around, as they return the energy with gracious smiles. One person comes forward with a powerful grace. It is a broad man, with white hair and a full beard, who is striking and burly. As Dr. Silver and Nurse Goode exit the craft, the man speaks to the couple, "Welcome, Calvin Wayne, Belle Cantrell, Anna Foster, Allegga and Igbogga Goleeka, and Zyus-Pahl and Whee-Pahl. I am Zeus."

"The same Zeus that came to Earth a few thousand of our years ago?" Calvin asks him.

"Yes, Calvin and we met some intelligent and inspiring humans. Of course, they needed our guidance. I was the Primary Soul of a world in your galaxy, as was my wife Hera and our companions, Apollo and Thor."

A younger man, also broad and handsome, has experienced eyes and a youthful physique. He comes from the crowd with a woman, whose elegant beauty is covered by a thin, but appropriate gown. The male speaks to the new residents, "I am Apollo, and this is Hera. We brought life to our worlds; plus the worlds we settled with that life. We thrived for many millions of years. Earth was a planet of wealth and great potential, but we watched it burn and create suffering for billions and billions of beautiful souls."

"That is all true. I will not deny that," Calvin nods.

Zeus is quick to reply, "We know that you and Belle and Anna are not responsible. Many people in your world, who were responsible, lived their lives without accountability and their lack of character cost lives. Since they controlled the means of production and the resources of your barbaric society, without learning any of life's hard lessons, they destroyed a paradise."

Another man among them, with blond hair and an impressive physique, approaches them and enters the discussion, "Greetings all. I am Thor. I also visited your world. We had a friendly bet to see whose society would win out: the Romans, Greeks, Vikings, Mayans, and the Hindus. Of course, with the Hindus, Oo and Ee were shown with a local projection so those Humans could see those Great Beings' power. So wonderful those people. Obviously, no one won on that world."

Apollo continues, "We want you to help us by traveling to vulnerable worlds, in peril, now or in the future, to help fix their trajectory. Like we did on Earth many years ago. As you have all traversed the whole of Existence, you can now decide to help save the lives and worlds of billions of people and infinite souls."

Calvin asks them, "Why don't we save our worlds? We learned that they were all destroyed. Can you help us save them?"

"Hello, I am Hera. We can help you fix your worlds and you can even return to them. Let's go eat and converse, in pleasure, before we go to the Grand Cathedral. There, the pool of infinity waits for us. From there, we can travel to any universe and enlighten any people to hopefully reaffirm their moral journey. And avoid a fate such as Planet Earth's, in nearly every dimensional rendition. Dr. Silver and Nurse Goode, are you going to join us, finally, and retire from the IAV Corps?" The woman leads the crowd along a path.

Dr. Silver looks at his wife, and they both smile. He and Nurse Goode tag along, and he replies, "We will this time. We enjoyed this group and have been thinking of retiring. We're ready. Thank you, Hera."

Calvin and Belle give the Ellagantce couple hugs, then join the crowd as they walk to the set of tables with food for all. Anna and Belle hug while in line for grub, and the nine travelers mingle, with the exalted folks, like they've all known each other for ages.

The group, of about forty people, enters the cathedral in a courteous manner. Maybe too slow for the impatient ones, but it's easy to develop patience in this universe. The crystal roof reflects and refracts the light from above. In the middle of the floor, a large, convex pool with images of stars, galaxies, and universes move around without direction.

Hera gets close to the edge of one side, holds her arms out over the portal, and declares, "Gurrea was caught in a star's supernova and Zor-ah was wiped clean by a meteor. Before those events occur, I will intercede. Let my hands take Gurrea." A visual of a glowing blue and gold planet moves into her hands, and she goes on, "I will move you to the healthy, warm zone of this lonely star." She moves the world into a fair system without a world.

Allegga and Igbogga smile, and Igbogga says, "Does this mean we can go back and be with all of our loved ones, but with our new healthy selves?"

Thor answers, "Yes, young Gurr, but you can stay here as long as you wish."

The Gurrs shake their heads, and Allegga says, "We want to go home, where we belong." Both become relieved and elated.

Hera continues, "Allegga and Igbogga Goleeka, whenever you wish to return home, it is there, waiting. You are healed and strong now, so your people may wonder why you will have an extended longevity." They hug their friends and walk to Hera, ready to leave. "When your loved ones are gone, both of you concentrate on this place, and you will return. Touch your world when you are ready."

The Gurrs hug the other passengers, and without regret, step close to Hera. As the world zooms closer, they both touch it with their fingertips...

SHLOOP!

Calvin's eyes go wide and he states, "I shouldn't be surprised by now." Belle smiles and nods.

Zyus-Pahl holds Whee-Pahl's hand as they walk to the exalted woman, and he says, "Are we next? Please tell me you can save our world!"

She replies, "Yes, of course." Hera spins the same galaxy around and lands with one specific star system on its outskirts. As they zoom in, a beautiful world comes into view, with ample greenery. She continues, "Yes, Zor-ah. Beautiful landscapes and the people of the Fair Horned race." As a meteor shoots towards the unwitting planet, Hera flicks it into an asteroid belt, where is creates a wave of collisions. She then projects a field of energy on the side of the planet that faces outer space. "You both ready?"

They both look at their friends and wave to the Humans and Ellagantce. Whee-Pahl wipes a tear from her eye. She says, "Yes, please take us home." The couple each put a hand on their world's image...

SHLOOP!

Hera turns to the Humans and says, "Earth, 21st Century, the origin of Calvin, Belle, and Anna, in the year 2030. Just over 25 years before the Last Dying, as the few survivors called it." A mass of nothing goes to her hands, then a universe spins and zooms to the Milky Way. Then to Earth, and finally to Washington, DC.

Zeus adds, "There is the current leader of the most powerful nation, giving a speech. They must listen or time will run out. Do the Human residents have wisdom for their planet? Perhaps an advanced technology we can provide to cut off the imbalance of power?"

"What if we supply the masses with a surplus of everything? Just hand them the technology of Instant Manufacturing, and we can make being greedy an obsolete sin," Belle remembers the early lessons.

"I doubt anything would sway the desire to enforce a cruel power over others. I might stay," Anna adds.

"Wait, I don't want to leave yet. Want to go in a little while? I would like to take a long vacation with Belle, if you want," Calvin asks Belle.

"Of course, let's stay awhile. Can we?" She asks them.

Hera nods, "Definitely." She waves her hands to lower the pool back to the calm circulation. She turns to the Humans, "You all can stay with us here as long as you wish, and you will be able to return to Earth, as well. Remember, if you really want to come back, just concentrate and focus on this place. Or, until you decide to become a Creator. We have plenty to do and whatever you want from your life, in the form of entertainment, is available here too."

Anna looks at Thor and they make eye contact. Thor walks to her as they look into each other's eyes, and she smiles, "I *am* staying here." She grabs Thor's arm. He smiles at her and they walk away, in a soft embrace.

Dr. Silver tells Anna before she is gone, "I see God smiles on Anna once more!" Anna throws a thumb up in the air.

"That's a tough bargain, Hera," Calvin scratches his scruffy chin.

"We have as much time as we want, Cal," Belle grabs his arm.

Calvin thinks, "I do want to go back and bring Instant Manufacturing. That's a great idea. We can bring that, and SOO to maybe take over the stock market?"

Belle likes the suggestion, "I'm in. Let's have fun."

Hera speaks again, "Then, you shall stay here with us, for now. We are a community, so we are all here to help each other."

"Let us go enjoy Heaven and the pleasures of this eternity," Zeus suggests to them.

The crowd clears out of the cathedral after Zeus speaks. As they exit the large, elegant structure, Dr. Silver and Nurse Goode stop them.

Dr. Silver speaks first, "Hey, you two, we're going to look around this universe for a new home, in total peace. We have thoroughly enjoyed our time with you, and if you want to see us, remember what Hera said about concentration: you can now travel back from Earth in 2030 to Heaven, but the same applies to this whole universe. We will be here, so you can travel to us directly."

Nurse Goode smiles and hugs Belle, "Belle, you are amazing and will be great here with Calvin. And, Calvin, it was a pleasure watching you heal and then, of course, you too fell for each other. Take care of all the souls you come across."

Calvin partially hugs Belle as they shake hands with the guides, "Thank you for everything. This was the adventure of a lifetime and I am truly grateful."

"Yes, Dr. Silver, thank you. This was a great honor and a blessing," Belle holds her heart as the two couples part. Belle and Calvin walk towards their new crowd as the doctor and nurse walk away on a path. In a flash, the Ellagantce couple disappear.

Calvin and Belle join their new community and receive a warm welcome on their way. Calvin pulls his spin-fidgeter out of his pants, and laughs, "Remember what I did with this? I can't believe what is going on. I thought we were in some grind of therapy, but..."

"I know, we have been through it all, so much, but now, it's all still so comforting and easy. Thank you for being the love of my life, Calvin."

"Thank you for being the love of all my Existence."

They stop on a stone bridge and embrace. Their kiss, so gentle and sweet, intensifies as he draws them together tightly. She throws her arms around him, and they zoom to a calm lake in the shadow of a light waterfall.

To My Mom,

You helped me keep my mind open against the Darkness

Thank you and I love you forever

To Everyone who has ever helped me or any other person
who suffers from illnesses and adversities,

Thank you for everything